AF430692

RAPPER'S DELIGHT

THE MOGUL SERIES BOOK ONE

KENYA GOREE-BELL

Illustrated by

WHIMSICAL DESIGNS LLC

Copyright © 2020 by Kenya Goree-Bell

All rights reserved.

No part of this book may be reproduced in any form or by any electronic or mechanical means, including information storage and retrieval systems, without written permission from the author, except for the use of brief quotations in a book review.

❀ Created with Vellum

For mom always for you

I never saw a wild thing sorry for itself. A small bird will drop frozen from a bough without ever having felt sorry for itself. ~ D. H. Lawrence

Oh but my joy today
    Is that we can all be proud to say
    To be young gifted and Black
    Is where it's at.
    ~Nina Simone

FOREWORD

Thank you for choosing Rapper's Delight!

I wanted to take a moment to share the following Content Warning.

This story contains gun violence, survivors remorse, loss of sibling, and love scenes that involve choking.

RAPPER'S DELIGHT

Get ready Book One of the Mogul Series

Tragedy separated them for twelve years…

Can they finally have the love promised?

Or will betrayal be their undoing.

Welcome to the world of The Mogul Series where the Young, Gifted and Black are met with intrigue and passion. Where fame is no guarantee of happiness but love may hold all the possibilities.

Meet Delightful Howard and FADE Carrington as they embark on a journey that promises passion as they try to reclaim what they lost in RAPPER'S DELIGHT.

FADE is the biggest rap star in the world and he has everything he ever wanted but his best friend's sister.

Delightful Howard is coming off the biggest win any writer can imagine but she will never rest until she knows all the secrets FADE holds.

Promises were made

Now it's time to deliver.

STOP. FUCKING. RUNNING.

Enter the world of The Mogul Series where smart women and ruthless men collide...

Power

Fame

Music

Passion

Justice Denied

12 YEARS BEFORE...

"Ok, I'm going to let you go with me but don't be acting so goo-goo eyed this time. It's super embarrassing seeing my sister looking at my best friend like he's her favorite caramel cupcake." Justice shook his head, looking at her so pitifully that Delightful couldn't help but attempt to smack the smirk from his lips one good time.

Leaping from her built-in wall desk, she almost had him too.

"Ha- ha! You missed shrimp!" He backed away with his arms shot forward in an attempt to ward her off. Try as she might Delightful knew that she would never reach Justice's face which at six-foot was way out of of her little five-foot swinging range.

"Don't worry punk, I got you," she huffed.

"Come-on, we need to get down there. FADE has already been blowing up my phone. That boy is a workaholic." Justice's grin took any censure out of his voice as he reached up and gripped the top of the door frame.

"You know you love it too. The music you guys make is hot, and it's important." Nodding to him as she walked past, she winked, "Who'd have thought y'all nerds were even capable of such coolness?" She winked at him, tucking her notebook into her bag.

"Carry this for me?" He canted his head, giving her his signature, "Do me this on solid," look that he knew she couldn't resist.

"Ok, but this is it. You're not weighing me down with your snacks." She rolled her eyes and swept past him and down the wide creaky stairs that led right into the parlor. The fact that they actually called it a parlor always made her giggle, mom insisted on it since that was what it was with its opening up to the dedicated living room. Her mom loved that room and everything about their century's old home so much she had a daddy to buy her a set of furniture that never got sat on which made daddy roll his eyes every time she chided anyone for sitting in there. Which is exactly what Delightful did as she sat down to lace up her Chucks.

"Oh, going with me has gone straight to your head, huh?" Justice shook his head his eyes rounded big like she'd lost her ever loving mind.

"Shhhh!" She hushed him and jumped up quick as she could making the plastic cover squeak.

"You better not be on my settee, Delightful!" mom called from somewhere in the back of the house.

"No ma'am," she called and licked her tongue out at Justice who ran a finger over his throat.

"You know she's going to come and check. You better make sure there isn't a booty print on there." He stood and stretched. Daddy called them growing pains. Justice hadn't seemed to stop growing since he turned fourteen and hit his growth spurt. He was constantly twisting this and turning, learning how to get comfortable in his ever changing body.

"Mommy, we're about to leave," he called over his shoulder once he'd finally settled.

"Be careful, stay out of those alleyways and call when you're about to leave. If it's late, I'll have your daddy pick you up when he gets home, so you won't have to walk." She patted his arm and turned her face so he could put a big smooch on her cheek.

"Daddy will be tired, mommy. We'll make it back fine and not too late."

"Umhm, you just want to spend time with Fernando. You ain't fooling anyone. Least of all me."

"I am not." Delightful sidled up and kissed the other cheek.

"Justice make sure your sister behaves." Their mother moved aside to let them pass. "And lock those bikes up, so they don't get stolen." She moved back to close the door then popped her head back out, "I know you sat on my settee, Delightful!"

"Sorry, mommy! Love you!" Delightful blew a kiss to her mother waving before gripping her handle bars to maneuver her bike behind her bother's as they road down the hill in front of the house before banking a left toward the housing community where FADE's family lived just beyond the football stadium. Their house stood in the shadow of the massive structure, but that never stopped the heat and blaze of the hot southern sun from hitting them at every turn. They pumped the peddles of the bikes down the hill, swerving and jumping curbs to reach their destination.

* * *

"Do you like it?" The deep timbre of FADE's voice hit Delightful so deep down and forbidden that she was lost for words. She looked up to the deep amber gaze reminiscent of the brandy her daddy drank on special occasions when Alabama won the National Championship. He was looking at her like her he was nervous, like he really cared what she thought about the music he and her brother had been working on for the last two hours.

"It's dope. I love it." She swallowed and dragged her eyes from him to look over to Justice, silently imploring him to save her from further mortification.

"She's right man, this one is good for radio and the club." Justice bopped his head, "Bring up the tempo a little bit, Ghad." He instructed the kid who nodded and manipulating the controls.

Delightful closed her eyes, losing herself in the music's flow, letting it wash over her in waves. She spun around in the office chair, humming to the music. She leaned her head back once she stopped spinning and opened her eyes. Her heart stopped. Fernando Anthony Duke Ellington Carrington, aka FADE — the most popular, most talented, the most everything boy at Garnet Senior High School was staring at her. Her heart could not take it. Then he laid that crooked smile on her. She squirmed. This was too much. Her heart was beating harder than the beat Ghadi was mixing.

"Are you going to prom, Delightful?" He eased off the wall where he'd been posted most of the evening and came to stand beside her chair.

"I… umm," Delightful was lost. Was he just asking or about to ask her?

"Nah, man. My pops ain't about to let Delightful go to the prom this year."

"He might if I take her. You want to go to the prom with me, baby?" He reached down and tugged her braid.

"Since when are you going to the prom, FADE? I thought you said it was whack?" Ghadi, whose name, Flower, their little sister told Delightful was supposed to be Ghandi, but the nurse left the N off his birth certificate chimed in as only he could-- completely out of order.

"Yeah, but I've changed my mind. So what's up Didi? You want to go to the prom with me or what?" He smiled at her then and the only thing she could do was smile and nod "Yes" because the words would not come. She thought they could be together fifty years and she would still find the words hard to come by whenever he smiled at her like that.

"You better ask my dad before your feelings get hurt," Justice advised giving his friend a hard look, "Don't make me kick your ass over my sister, bro."

"Nah, man, it's cool, I have sisters too. I'd fuck a bitch up over Flower and Willow. Trust that." He tipped his head to acknowledge his friend.

"Yup, yup," Ghadi called from where he was mixing a new sequence of percussions, "Straight up murder."

Everyone laughed, knowing good and well that Ghadi was always the first to make peace. Even at fifteen, he showed more wisdom than most adults. Stopping fights and brokering peace had gotten him the moniker 'Ghad of Peace'.

Both boys had been offered elite scholarships along with Justice to a private boarding school on the other side of town, but they had all chosen to stay at their beloved high school. Delightful wished they'd went. She definitely would have gone to Southern Ivy Academy if she had that opportunity. She was a hard worker, but she *had to work* that was her gift as her mom often told her Justice's and her younger sisters were just more apparent with Justice's poetry, Lovie-Belle's writing and Miracle's photographic memory.

On the way to FADE's house, they saw that it was getting increasingly worse in the neighborhood. Word around the neighborhood was gangs from up north were infiltrating the area. The community was besieged on one side by constant policing and the other by emerging gangs.

She knew that this was a powder keg ready to explode. Her family was up the hill a few blocks away, but it may as well have been another planet. She knew FADE's parents were talking about moving. They were torn because their dad was the pastor of the neighborhood church and he felt that it was part of his ministry to live in the community.

Looking at their mother this afternoon talking about a recent encounter she had with some boys hanging out on the corner made Delightful think his stance wouldn't hold long. She hoped they moved up on the hill near them. It was way safer and then she could see FADE more. It would be so awesome if they could live next door instead of her eccentric cousins, but she knew that would never happen. Their house was even older than hers and they claimed it had been in the family since freedom, so no one was moving out of "The Love Palace". She went over there but never stayed long because they weren't being supervised properly since their parents tragic "accident" and only their great-grandma on their daddy's side was watching them and she made money by selling moonshine her mom said. She knew her mom would have no problem with her visiting the Carrington house if they moved up by them since their daddy was a preacher and all.

"Hey my little daydreamer, you ready? I'm going to ride up with y'all to ask your dad about prom." He pulled her out of the chair. With a quick look over her shoulder, she glimpsed that Justice and Ghadi had gathered their things and were heading out. Her body came flush with his. She knew she should step back but didn't.

He slouched down to her level, and she leaned into him. He felt so hard — all wiry muscle. He had to lean down because he was taller than Justice, she'd say around six-two. His skin was the color of crushed topaz, almost golden in hue, his locks swirly. He was probably the most beautiful thing that she'd ever seen and had thought so from the moment he entered her home to play Xbox with her brother when she was eight. She had loved him from day one and could never think of a time when she wouldn't. And the icing on the caramel cupcake that Justice teased her about was he smelled so dang good. It was not a stinky, over-the-counter scent. It was just him being exceptionally clean. She closed her eyes and inhaled, taking in as much of him as she could.

"Can I kiss you, Didi? I really have been wanting to kiss you for a while now." His words were whispered soft in her ear and it made her shiver. She felt her body respond almost painfully.

"I promise only a kiss. Is that ok?" He tilted her chin up and looked into her eyes.

"Why now?" Her voice sounded like a whisper to her own ears because she knew he was well aware how much she liked him.

"I had to make sure Justice was cool with us being together." His eyes darted to the door as he lowered his voice which seem to rub along the inside of her body leaving cinders in its wake.

"Oh, really?" She quirked her eyebrow in challenge. "You had to get his permission?"

"Yeah," He eyes slid away like the spot on her neck was a magnet he couldn't drag his eyes away from.

"Because you didn't want to ruin your friendship over a girl, you were just dating for a while?" She stepped back. He stepped forward now she was pressed against the desk with him a wall in front of her. She exhaled, and her chest rubbed against him. He took a quick step back. He was just light enough that she could see the blush infuse his face.

"You know he would never go for that. He grilled me. I had to be honest." His gaze was raw. Imploring.

"So what made him say ok?' She crossed her arms tilting her chin up, wondering how upset she should be that her brother felt it was his duty to manage her dating life.

"I told him..." He cleared his throat and threw his head back and sighed, scrunching his eyes closed tightly exhaling. Her eyes went straight to the corded muscles in his throat. She was going to like kissing him there. She bit her lip at the naughty thought. After he took a couple deep breaths, he steadied his feet and cupped her face in his big hands. "I told him that this is the beginning of forever, Delightful. You and me — this is forever."

"FADE." She cupped her hands around his neck and brought his lips to hers. For years she'd dreamed of kissing FADE. He was her crush, her brother's best friend, and at this moment Delightful could not be bothered to care because kissing FADE was better than any caramel cupcake.

* * *

"Mom said not to go in the alleyway." Delightful caught up with Justice and grabbed his arm when he turned his bike into the corridor.

"Yeah and she told you to behave but I know you were kissing FADE just now." He winked at her and laughed when she smacked his arm.

"Yeah, and we need to talk about how you think folks have to check with you before asking me out." She poked his chest, putting her foot back on the peddle.

"Right because you're my kid sis and I look out for you." He was so unapologetic and proud that she couldn't help but shake her head at his tone.

"Oh, and like you don't kiss and do more with Lyric? She

doesn't have a big brother to look out for her." She countered, daring him to deny it.

"She doesn't need one, we've been together since six grade. I'm marrying her as soon as I graduate." He held his hands up like so what before grabbing the handlebars again. "Then we are going on tour. To get our music out."

"What about school?" her voice raised at news he had been holding out on.

"What about it?" He scrunched up his face.

"Boy, mom and daddy are going to be so mad at you if you pass up a music scholarship to go on the road and run off and marry Lyric!" Her eyes darted to FADE who been at the mouth of the ally stopped and looked back to them.

"Did you know about this FADE?" His immediately closed off expression told her everything she needed to know. "Oh, you're in on it too. No wonder y'all have had this mad rush to make music."

"Listen, Delightful. There is something you have to understand. When you have a gift like mine and what FADE has, you can't be boxed in. A promoter with the summer music festivals contacted us after seeing one of our YouTube videos and offered us a spot. We'll be back before school starts." He patted her on the shoulder and turned away from her back toward the alley.

"Ugh! You know you had me thinking the worst." She followed behind them, who were both laughing at her upset.

"Hey Mr. Vaughn!" They all called to the dapper little man who owned the last penny store in the neighborhood. He waved to them as he walked by, leaning on his cane.

They picked up speed as they flew to through the neighborhood. Three blurs picking up wind and air as they laughed and swerved over sidewalks and jumped curbs. Justice was flying ahead with FADE hanging back just enough to give her the occasional wink.

The sound when it came blasted like bombs had been set off right in their faces. She crashed into FADE. The bikes were tangled. She was on top of FADE, who had taken the brunt of the fall. Her arm from wrist to elbow felt like it was on fire. She looked and saw the skin was flayed from her arm. The pain was blinding. Tears stung her eyes and her breath sawed in and out like she had just done a fifty meter dash. She heard a groan under her and untangled herself from FADE, pulling her now useless bike away from her. She looked down as he eased up there was blood all over his back. "Oh my God, FADE, are you ok?" She sounded like she was screaming to her own ears.

"I'm..." She saw all the color drain from his face and followed his gaze.

"JUSTICE!" They both screamed and ran limping to the prone body of her brother.

She already knew as she knelt down before him by the weird angle his body lay. His chest was a mass of red. The things that sounded like bombs going off were bullets tearing through her brother's chest. He was gasping for air. Yet every breath he took made more blood gush out.

"Justice, I love you. I love you, Justice."

"I love you, Delightful." He gasped then looked to FADE, "T-Take care of 'em."

"I got you man," Delightful felt hot tears roll down her cheeks as she watched as FADE sobbed touching his head to her brother's. They keep telling him that he was loved, and prayed for the Lord to keep him long after he was gone.

CHAPTER 1

*N*o Justice, No Peace

12 Years Later...

"FADE is going to be in here." Lovie-Belle quirked her eyebrow at Delightful, reapplying her lipstick as the limousine pulled up to the curb to await its turn to deposit them on the red carpet.

"I don't see how we can avoid it." Delightful picked up her crystal covered clutch and dug out a compact to check her lipstick smiling into the mini mirror to make sure she didn't have lip gloss smudges on her teeth. "The studio thought it was such great PR having a connection with Creative Chaos, since the story hinted at their beginnings." She glanced up, sarcasm dripping from every word, saw the look her sister was giving her and snapped the compact close. "What?" She sighed, getting ready for the argument they'd had million times.

"You. You want to avoid him. You don't want to have

anything to do with him. And you won't tell us why. You need to stop blaming FADE, Delightful." Lovie-Belle huffed just as the door opened. "But don't worry I have your back, let the shunning continue." She threw over her shoulder as the attendant reached in to help her out the car because loyalty above everything in public even if they called each other on it in private was their creed.

Delightful rolled her eyes in, "I'll be damned if I do", as the door on her side opened and a strong brown hand reached in for her. She grasped it and stepped out into the flashing bulbs and happy screaming fans.

She couldn't help it, she loved it. She earned this and deserved every accolade that she and her sister received for their Best Original Screenplay Oscar, and she was determined to bask in it. She would not let thoughts of FADE's treachery affect her tonight. Tonight was about Justice, his story, "JUST US" a movie about the love and loyalty of a big brother for his sisters who's life had been taken too soon. Critics called it the most important film on gun violence and a movie that spoke for a generation.

This was her life's work. At first she hadn't thought beyond just getting his story out as it burned a hole in her heart. Now the possibilities were endless. No one was more shocked than Lovie-Belle and her when their passion project first got accepted and then green lit for a movie.

They took what they prepared and grabbed that opportunity with both hands. There was nothing they couldn't do now. The studio wanted her to make a companion piece about FADE's rise highlighting the pitfalls and the promise of hip hop. Up til now his rise had been swathed in mystery and he kept it that way. They felt with their shared history he would be willing to grant her the right to tell his story. She knew that is why they engineered this party with Creative Chaos to get her and FADE in the same room, something she had avoided since her brother's funeral and she realized that he was part of the reason Justice was killed if not out right responsible for it. The executives and Lovie-Belle thought she was was being petty for not wanting to do it.

Walking around the car, she grasped her sister's hand and walked the red carpet, stopping to sign autographs and take pictures with fans. There were a lot of little girls in the crowd and they made sure to take pictures with everyone who asked. She didn't care if the paparazzi planted some. She wanted to make someone's day if she could. Seeing the shining excitement in some of the kid's eyes, she couldn't resist posing with them for their Instagram stories. This was the night that almost all of her dreams had come true. The only thing missing was Justice. He should be here had whispered in her ear all night and since the nomination. She missed him so much that her soul ached with it sometimes.

"Whew, it feels better in here. There was no breeze out there, despite all those strategically placed fans. They only blew hot heat. They should've had those misters like at Disney World," Lovie-Bell groused, dabbing at her forehead with a handkerchief.

"So, you're just going to tell folks how to run their red carpets, huh?" Delightful laughed at her sister as they walked into the crush of actors, studio heads, and various famous people at the Creative Chaos Oscar Party, FADE's company — named after the group he and her brother founded. She wanted to scream every time she heard the name. It was the name they settled on the very day Justice died. The link couldn't be ignored in the movie. The screen play they wrote, and now the studio wanted to work with Creative Chaos who had long since branched out from just hip hop into creating sounds for all manner of things from movies, toys, video games and even phones.

They held several patents dealing with sound mixing and

secret algorithms on the tech side. There was no way to not deal with them in making music. They had received their own Oscars for sound and tech at an event held earlier in the week. It surprised no one. They were leading the way in so many spheres. She couldn't begrudge them their success. She and her sister's had found their own. She only wished that Justice was here to be part of this and she would never feel okay with him not.

"Oh, there you are! I'm so glad that you could make it." Delightful looked over to see a little sprite of a woman with long curly hair that reached nearly to her waist.

"Wow, Flower, is that you?" Lovie-Belle slipped between them to hug the woman.

"It is I. How are you guys doing? I bet great, huh? Like totally walking on sunshine!" She beamed a beautiful smile over to them that Delightful couldn't help but respond to. Flower was herself, as always, a bottle of sunshine. She brightened up every room. People were surprised that someone so kind took no prisoners when it came to being the COO of Creative Chaos. Everyone knew that no one got to FADE or Ghadi without first getting permission from Flower. She was a power in her own right and Delightful respected her and her loyalty. It was her brother's that she questioned.

"Yes, it is pretty fantastic," she smiled back as they made their way further into the room. The party was was in full swing. Every tier of celebrity and fame-monger was present. The Creative Chaos party was the hottest ticket of the night beside the Oscars themselves. There was not a studio executive or agent worth his salt not present.

They had the soundtrack on rotation. The beat throbbing with the light made the room seem to vibrate with FADE, Justice, Ghadi's signature beats that they created that night so long ago. The emotions of hearing her brother's music was bittersweet.

"Come on, Delightful, let go dance for Justice!" Flower clapped with glee, leading them to the middle of the dance floor. The crowd parting for her like she was a general heading to the front lines.

Turning away was not an option and Delightful found that she wanted to honor her brother by dancing to his music. The women laughed and threw their hands up in celebration of the triumph they had on behalf of their brother. Giving herself over to the rhythm and beat Delightful laughed even as her heart clinched loving what FADE had done with the music they'd created. He'd modernized the songs but kept the essence and truth of Justice's verses. Hearing the voice of Justice's girlfriend, Lyric made her smile as the artist sang and rapped with the irreverence of her nature as she brought to life who Justice was just as she promised she would when Flower asked her to be on the soundtrack.

Looking at her sister and Flower dancing around her felt just like the many girls' only parties they'd had growing up. It seemed as if everything else fell away and it was just the friends enjoying each other and staying up way too late on a Saturday.

"And now a let's slow it down…" the women looked at each other as the first strands of the old school, "Simply Beautiful" by Al Green, the best version in Delightful's opinion began to play. They grinned and begin to edge off the dance floor. "You know who loves this song, don't you?" She looked into Flower's delighted gaze, puzzled. "My brother," she whispered as she turned Delightful around to look into the amber gaze of the boy she loved twelve years ago. He was all man now.

Everything fell away. There was nothing but Mr. Green

promising all the things he could do and FADE standing before her with that same promise in his eyes. His look promised so much — passion and retribution. Delightful wobbled as she felt air at her back with her sister and friend, leaving her there to finally face FADE.

He took a step, then another toward her as if giving her time to run from him if she wanted to. His looked dared her. He was a panther walking toward her and somehow she knew if she didn't flee he would never let her go again. His purpose was in every step he took in her direction. She didn't know why she couldn't. It wasn't fear. It wasn't hatred but some other unnamable force that compelled her. The compulsion over-road every instinct she had except the one that always wanted him. Now it was crystal clear to her why she never wanted to see him. The war raging inside of her was one she was destined to lose — the first few battles, anyway.

It seemed as if her feet were glued to the floor, but she couldn't budge when he moved in and took her into his arms. He wrapped his arms around her waist and pulled her close. Her breath caught. His body was all steel corded muscle. There was nothing soft about him. Every part of him was a promise. He towered over her but somehow made sure that their bodies touched in all the right places. Her arms slid up over his broad shoulders and he rocked and swayed with her. He'd taken off his jacket, and he wore two very thin chains that had medallions that she couldn't make out before she was nose to chest with him. He rubbed low circles on her back like he was well aware of what she liked. Her eyes closed against the scent of him.

He was so fucking lickable. Dammit. How was he still having this effect on her? Her body's response was a squish and slide coupled with a clinch and an ache that only he could assuage. He promised to please with every movement he made that caused his dick to brush against her. Their bodies were in sync with the music and each other. She felt him shudder and knew he was not unaffected. He felt it too. His reaction was more than evident pressed against her. She never wanted it to end, and she hated herself for that. She hated him, too. Could you come from dancing like this, she wondered. She felt damn close. If she pressed closer, she'd be right there. She panted. He groaned and leaned down, pulling her closer. "Come with me." Then he looked up and winked in that devilish way of his and pulled her behind him out of the throng of people.

CHAPTER 2

*J*ust Forever

FADE DIDN'T KNOW if he wanted to choke her or fuck her. He'd probably end up doing both as soon as he got the chance if he was completely honest. He didn't release his grip on her, not leaving the party, not going up the back stairs to the private room he'd secured as soon as he knew she'd be in attendance, nor when she stood before him like a gazelle about to be captured in the jaws of a lion. He'd never let her go if he had the chance. Twelve fucking years he'd been without his best friend and twelve years she'd evaded him at every turn. Refusing to see him and going so far as to move cross-country, he knew to get away from him. He wanted to know why. Why had she run from him? He had not only lost Justice, but he'd lost her by her own design and he never understood her reasons for doing him like that. Delightful had left a gigantic gaping hole in his life and his heart. He wrestled with the anger that threatened to poison every touch. He was determined to touch her and if she let him. He was going to blow her fucking mind. No more hiding. Tonight would be her reckoning.

"What is this about FADE?" She pulled her hand out of his grasp and turned to look at him. The fact that she would dare ask him that question sent a spiral of cold rage through him he had long thought conquered. He inhaled slowly, tying to reclaim his calm and failed instead, allowing the coldness that he'd become synonymous with to lace every word.

"I don't know Didi maybe the fact that you dared show your face to me and stopped acting the coward after twelve years made me think finally you were ready to keep your promise."

"What promise?" She scoffed then stepped to him, acid dripping from every word, "And nobody calls me Didi anymore."

He turned away from her. The rage that continued to lick at him and the hurt her words caused as they cut through him made his hands curl into a tight fist. Breathe. He closed his eyes against the pain and fury her words wrought. "I was the only one to ever call you that." The words barely got through the clench of his jaw. He felt the pulse ticking there, knew she could see and by the flashing response of her eyes knew she didn't give a damn. Damn, that made his dick hard. He was going to enjoy tangling with her. He'd teach her to put those claws to better use.

"Oh, well." She shrugged like some little tough punk trying to start a fight. He chuckled, realizing that's exactly what she wanted. For them to crash and burn before they had a chance to burn together. He caught the wariness in her eyes. He allowed a slow smile to spread across his face. He waited, he was damn good at waiting. He'd been forced to wait for twelve years.

"Oh, so you're tough now?" he quizzed, stalking slowly over to her. He was known for his patience. He'd wait. He knew by the way her pulse fluttered that she wouldn't be able to. He wondered how long her patience would last. When she was younger, she was never good at that. Impulsive. Had she grown out of it? The heel tapping gave her away. If she fled, he'd follow and if she stayed, she'd be beneath him.

"I had to be. Watching my brother die did that." She stuck her chin out in challenge. One he'd been twelve years ready to accept. *Little girl, you don't know how ready I am for your sass,* he thought gripping her chin. "You'en have to be tough had you let me in, Delightful. I would've had you from day one. My whole family — hell, most people in the community. You didn't have to be alone then and you don't have to be alone now." His words sounded gruff to his own ears. He was way past playing games, and he had never played games with her.

"Why in the hell would I come to you, FADE? After what you did?" She slapped his hand away and backed up, shaking her head at him, her own rage in every step she took away from him.

Dread crawled up his throat. As he watched her look at him as if he were a monster. Then she rounded on him. "The streets were talking after they killed my brother. What were you mixed up in? Why did y'all move so soon after? Yeah, your music blew up and you were hot but not New York hot. Why the big move with your entire family? What were you running from?"

Relief swamped him. She was guessing. She didn't know the truth — could never know. Telling her would only put a price on her head because one thing he knew about Delightful, she would not let it go. She would turn over the heaviest rock and lift that burden as if it were a feather if it meant bringing what she thought was retribution to the wrong done to Justice. He couldn't let that happen and he'd done too much already to make sure she was far away from people and situations that would do her harm, so he kept to the story he'd created all those years ago when reporters first began to ask his origin story.

"I had to be in the studio, Didi. I was given time based on beats Ghadi and I created. That helped us seed Creative Chaos into an indie label. Not sexy, just hard work."

Her blink was slow as she assessed what he'd just told her and he could tell she wasn't buying it. "I know the party line, but you're not fooling me. Somebody laid in wait and shot at us. Folks said that you knew about it."

He felt like he'd been sucker punched. All this time he thought it was survivor's remorse when in fact she blamed him. His eyes stung. He felt panic rise inside his body and acid ride high in his throat. That she would actually think… Rage ticked in his jaw again, swelled deep in his spirit, eased into his heart with an icy fury that he held tight to a leash. Twelve years of therapy withered under the accusation she made. He wanted to lash out, to go to his base self, let his id rise, conquer and lay waste to everything in his view. Her. Her nerve to stand there and utter those words — words that would mean death to anyone else who'd dared utter them, sliced through his heart.

"Get out." He ground out as he stalked to the leather couch, flung his body against the cushions and threw his arm over his eyes, trying to get his breathing under control. Years of therapy and coming to terms with his own guilt around Justice's death had not prepared him for the accusation still ringing in his ears from the woman he'd thought of every day for twelve years. So much time wasted on a person who obviously hated him. Fuck his life! He was stunned.

"Go on, little girl before you find yourself in a tougher situation than you thought. Go enjoy your party. You won't see me again," he growled, knowing he was teetering on the edge of a very dark place. A place he wanted no one to see. The darkness he'd struggled with since loosing his best friend and the only promise of real happiness he ever had. Which stood before him now with accusations dropping like bombs from her beautiful lips. He just needed to shut it all out for a moment, to give him enough time to get his shit together. He couldn't do with her here. He never wanted her to see him like that — not now. He would never find a safe place with her thinking him complicit in Justice's death.

"Well, see, that's the problem. The studio wants another movie, a companion piece about your rise to fame." He sat up at her words. He must have let his true feelings bleed through because she stepped back.

"Let me get this straight they want Lovie-Belle and you to write and direct it. Aw, hell nah." He leaned back and chuckled rawly into the arm he covered his face with again. Un-fucking-believable.

"Let me tell you something, FADE. This was not my idea. I really don't care but if you think with the questions that arose from my film swirling all over social media and in the press that your IPO launch is going to go smoothly you may want to rethink that." She tapped her foot like she had him by the balls.

"Thanks to the creative license you took. I could have sued you, Delightful. My lawyers told me to and I would've won. I decided to honor Justice's wishes though and look out for you. Now you're trying to blackmail me into telling a story I never wanted told in the first place. You are fucking incredible, lady." He shook his head not bothering to look up at her hoping she'd just leave so he could go on with pulling his life back together after her own brand of chaos had been unleashed in his life.

Instead, he heard the click of her heels as she walked over closer as if he were some type of child to be toyed with. She was taunting a lion that had been starved—had never had his hunger sated from the first time he claimed her all those years ago. Then she decided to sashay her little ass right on over to him. Tempting him after slicing him with her words so deep that he had to lie down like a debutante on a fainting couch to gather himself after her vicious attack. Like any wounded animal, he still had fight in him. So when she demanded, "FADE look at me." He did and reached up quick as any natural predator on their home turf and pulled her down on top of him.

Her reckoning was at hand.

* * *

DELIGHTFUL GASPED as her body hit the hard expanse of FADE's chiseled chest. Her hands were crushed between them, but he gave her enough space to get them free. That was it, though. His arms were clamped around her like a vise. His breath was even, but his eyes were cold. Rage poured off him in chilly waves. Her breasts were pressed against him. With each breath they both took, the thin material covering her brushed against him as her nipples grazed him. They hardened. If he noticed he ignored it. His angry gaze never left hers.

"You don't listen do you?" he whispered down to her.

"Not if I can help it. Doing what other people want rarely gets you what you want," She winked and smiled at him.

He barked a laugh at her. "Quoting my lyrics back at me." He shook his head, smiling despite himself.

"They are great lyrics and it's true." She shrugged and watched as the light dimmed in his eyes. The mask was back.

"Then you won't be surprised when I don't give you want you want." His arms loosened enough for her to move away, but she didn't. She stayed, interlacing her fingers and resting her chin on them atop his chest. She looked into those amber eyes that she missed even as she cursed herself for still finding them beautiful.

"It's not what I want. Lovie-Belle wants this and I'm doing this for her. Her dream is to be the next big writer-director and any project I'm attached to has a clause that includes her." She could feel his deep sigh at her words.

"This is a win, FADE. After this you can consider yourself free from any promises, you made Justice." Her voice drifted off as she saw his lips curl into a sneer.

"Promises I made to Justice have nothing to do with you. You don't determine when I feel my obligation is over." His gaze pierced her like icy fire, and he moved his arms back around her pulling her closer. "Especially when you can't remember your own." Anger and something more darkened his eyes. She pressed her hands against his chest and felt the hard beat of his heart thrumming against her fingers. Her breath caught, thinking back to that day when he'd said, "Forever".

"The f—," her words were muffled by the delicious onslaught of his lips and Delightful knew there was nothing that she could do to stop him. She was lost in his taste, the feel of his arms enveloping her just tight enough for her to know that he was never letting her go. He was a wonderful kisser the first time, but age and experience had made him a master. The way he slid his tongue against hers, swirled then sucked it into his mouth, teasing then testing her limits sent a trill straight to her pussy. Then he delved his tongue in slowly at first, tentative almost asking, seeking her acquiesce. His hand cupped her neck as he slanted his mouth over hers. The kiss exploded. Hot fire raced through her. Her panties drenched as her hips ground against the hard ridge of his dick. All thoughts of retribution fled. Only the promise that was seeded over a decade ago. The forever promise that they sealed with a kiss. That they promised now, though no words were spoken. In truth words weren't needed because their bodies spoke for them. Their limbs tangled. Delightful semi-straddled him. His dick hung to the right, so she felt the full force of him as she rubbed against him. He grabbed her ass, rucking up her dress. He groaned against her lips when he touched her. "You're so fucking wet, I knew you'd be wet for me." His head dipped down as he sucked the skin at the hollow of her neck into his mouth. His hands urged her on as she rode his dick through his pants. Delightful gasped as two long fingers pressed inside of her. She didn't know which sensation she wanted to chase. His fingers or the hardness teasing her clit. She needn't have worried because FADE came to the rescue, angling himself just so that his fingers worked her in tandem to his thrusting hips. "That's it Didi, I want you come to for me." She moaned, dipping her head down into his chest, helpless to stop. Powerless to do anything other than what he commanded as he continued to urge her on as she worked herself against his hardness. "You're going to make me come too. I can feel that hot little pussy." His hips gyrated as his fingers fucked deep into her pressing her G-spot. Delightful cried out as pleasure pulsed through her body from the simultaneous orgasms overtaking her body.

With trembling fingers she reached between them and unzipped his pants and released his long thick dick. Sitting back on her hunches she wrap on hand at the base and the other at the crown. Her hand was slick with the pre-cum seeping from him. Keeping her movements steady, she glided over the head and back down, repeating her rhythm, watching him as he watched her. Her thighs clinched at the sight of him with his hips arching as he fucked himself into her hands, slamming into them over and over again until his seed shot from him in a magnificent arch.

"Damn," he sighed falling back on the couch pulling her into his arms.

"Just Forever," he whispered kissing the top of her head

"What?" She looked up at him.

"That's what I want the movie named." The way he looked down at her made Delightful feel like he was speaking about way more than a movie.

CHAPTER 3

ust For Now

SHE COULDN'T BELIEVE she allowed him to touch her... She couldn't believe she actually liked — no, loved every freaking moment of it. He'd had her begging him. Shame unfurled inside of her like sticky tar clinging to every pore. Delightful slid her eyes across the dash and glimpsed the muscular hands gripping the steering wheel. She had to stifle the groan that bubbled up inside of her as she remembered how those long fingers felt as they brought her to climax over and over again.

"What's on your mind, Didi?" She could tell by the way his eyebrow quirked that he already knew the answer. Smug ass.

"Nothing," she cleared her throat, deliberately turning her body away from his as she saw the city lights as a blur as they sped by. Why had she agreed to let him see her back to her hotel? UGH! She was dumb. He had agreed to the deal, had even made a title request. Still, she needed to have that solidified. This project was important to Lovie-Belle, and she knew that she would finally get to the bottom of what happened to Justice if FADE agreed to the let them make a movie about his start in Hip Hop. She was determined to find away to bring peace to her family for her brother's senseless death.

"C'mon, I can see something is bothering you." Impatience rang in every word as he pulled into the private entrance of the boutique styled hotel she and her sister decided to stay for the time they were in L.A. She couldn't wait to get back to their little bungalow right outside of Berkeley, where they had all went to college, she and Lovie-Belle both went to film school there and Miracle, their younger sister was still in a graduate program. They'd stayed for Miracle, the little ingrate who'd moved out last year because in her words along with an exasperated eye-roll they hovered too much. She was a carefree, Autistic girl, and they were killing her vibe, she claimed.

He pulled the car in and got out, though there was a valet at this entrance as well as the front. The hotel catered to a very select clientele, and they wanted every need of the guests seen to.

She could feel his anger. She wondered why she cared. She looked over at him.

"You're not coming up." She looked up at him as he stood behind the door, holding it open for her.

"Oh, yeah?" He quirked an eyebrow at her before stepping back, holding the door wider as she stood to get out.

"Nope." She looked up at him. His eyes were turbulent. She saw the storm of emotions raging in his eyes, there was no easy going facade he showed her, no that was for the world. His fans who believed he was so chill never getting into beefs with other artists. Having a reputation as being too lofty to belittle himself with chumps, who dared to challenge him. He settled all of that in the studio, rapping harder than anyone else, putting out albums consistently and reaping the benefits. 'Never faded' was his mantra. If they saw him now that image would be shattered because now he seethed with rage. For her he showed her the real FADE. She stepped closer, her instinct to soothe him outweighing everything else.

He grabbed her and pulled her into his arms. He bent his head, waiting for her to meet him. She touched her lips to his. That was all it took for him to claim her. His mouth was hot and his taste delicious, the smokiness of the whiskey he drank earlier mixed with the flavor that was all his own. Their tongues battled, slid and sucked. She became lost in him. He held her so close, as if he couldn't bear to let her go. She felt herself melting for him. She loved how they fit. He was all wiry muscle and hard everywhere. She could feel the hard edge of his dick pressing against her.

"Let me come up, Delightful. Let me make love to you tonight." He urged once he pulled away and pressed a soft kiss on her forehead.

"I can't." She shook her head. "Lovie-Belle is coming back and we are in the same room."

He eased back, his eyes slitted in disappointment. "Cool, send me the pre-production schedule and we can work everything out. I'm heading out for New York first thing."

"Oh, so you were just going to hit it and quit it?" She smirked and moved out of his arms and turned away.

"No." He'd already pulled her back against his body. "I already told you what this was. Stop playing." His hand curved around her neck and the whispered words brushed against her ear before he licked the back of her lobe and gently sucked the flesh into his mouth. He pressed closer, so she felt every hard line of him. "This isn't a game. I'm done waiting."

He stepped back and her legs were so weak from the overwhelming need he'd created that she stumbled forward and would have fallen if he'd not caught her and steadied her. She turned back and speared him with her wrath, snatching her hand away as if burned.

"I'm not playing. I've been very clear about what my intentions are. This is about the movie and Justice's legacy."

"Really?" He scoffed. "You've handled Justice's legacy, Delightful, and already used my name to do it. You can tell yourself that this is about Lovie-Belle, Justice or whatever you need to make wanting to be with me palatable. Know this you've wasted years running from me and you're about to find out it was for nothing."

She swung her clutch negligently in her hand for a long moment. "What I know for sure, Fernando Anthony Duke Ellington Carrington is this, you have been hiding something and I will find out what it is."

* * *

"So you are sure he said he was onboard with the project and he wanted it named, 'Just Forever'? Why that name? The studio's going to want to run that through focus groups before they approve that."

Delightful watched as her sister worried her lip, nibbling it to death as they sat on the balcony of their small bungalow eating breakfast. It was way too early for this drama. She hadn't even had her coffee this morning, and she had no desire to go back over this for the hundredth time. Which she knew she would until FADE decided to set up a meeting or call them and say it was a no go.

There was nothing in writing, so he was not obligated to them in any way. She only had his word. She scoffed, thinking of the way he lambasted her by not remembering their promise. He was dead wrong she'd never forgot that promise. It had only changed for her once Justice died. The forever promise for her would always mean her loyalty to her brother. That's who she owed her forever to now. The boy who never had a chance to live his dream. The boy who was everything good in this word. The one possibly betrayed by his best friend.

With that thought shame claimed her again as she thought of how she melted for FADE like a bebop dropped on the hot Alabama asphalt.

"What's with that look, Delightful?" Love-Belle mumbled around the piece of blueberry muffin she'd just buttered and popped into her mouth.

"Nothing," Delightful sighed, avoiding the probing look her sister gave her.

"Well, that's a lie if I ever…" She cut off as The Walking Dead themed music chimed.

"It's time for you to change that," she scoffed getting up from the table taking their breakfast plates with her.

"You're still mad that you got they killed off Carl," Delightful laughed picking up her phone glancing at the unknown number before putting it back on the table.

"Yeah, and your ass is really is the Governor," Lovie-Bell huffed closing the door behind her.

"Hater-jealous because I'm Michonne," She laughed just as voice mail lit up. She hit replay and almost dropped her phone when she heard his voice come through the speaker, all rough and sexy with sleep.

"Hey, Didi. I just got back in. I'm staying out in Malibu at my friend's Sadiq's place. We want y'all to come out here so we can work out the details. Hasan, Sadiq's brother, has already talked with the studio about them heading the production team. So, we're good as soon as we hear back from you and Lovie-Bell. I can't wait to see you."

"Wait what did I just hear?" Lovie-Bell's near screech had Delightful swiveling her head catching her sister's gaze. "Why did he say he can't wait to see you all sexy like?"

Delightful tore her guilt-ridden gaze away from her sister's, but it was too late.

"I knew it! Something happened between you two, didn't it? Ohmygosh!!! You and FADE?" Delightful leaned back to watch the giddy display of her sister shimmying with the air.

"Calm down, it's not that deep." She stood, moving past her into the kitchen.

"What happened then?" Lovie-Belle slid the door close and faced her.

Delightful took her time placing her coffee cup on the counter. "We kissed."

"And?" Lovie-Bell proved to Delightful in that moment exactly why she regretted ever begging her mother for a baby sister.

"A little bit of other stuff. Now mind your business and go pack because getting all the way out to Malibu in traffic is going to be headache enough." She watched her sister huff away, knowing her desire to see this project done would override her nosiness, for now at least. Picking up her phone, she pressed the last number.

"Hey, Didi." She rolled her eyes at the way her heart skipped when he called her that name.

"I just talked to Lovie-Bell, it may take us a minute to get out there." She said in a matter-of-fact way, trying to remove all familiarity from her voice and the sparks of desire that came along with the rough sound of his voice.

"We figured. Sadiq got your address from the studio so the car service should be there in half an hour to bring you guys out." He sounded so chill. She envied him that. She always was on the go. A doer. Being gifted the way he was just made things easier. She was a screenwriter, but she'd always felt she'd had to work for it. She knew FADE worked hard, yet even when they were kids music just seemed to pour from him, Ghadi and Justice. The same was true for Lovie-Belle and Miracle, their gifts were given at birth her gift was being a hard worker. "I don't know if I should be like wow, thanks for going to so much trouble for us, or mad because you being so highhanded," she mused, headed back to her office that had been Miracle's bedroom prior to her moving out.

"I won't tell you how you should be as long as you get here. Bring enough for the weekend. We have a lot of work to do and need a fast turnaround."

"Highhanded," she snapped, shoving her laptop into her backpack. She hated purses, so this was always her default, much to Lovie-Belle's dismay, who loved nothing better than a snazzy purse.

"Assertive and smart. You forget this movie you want to make is about me. Folks have been after me for years to make a movie, do a documentary or let them follow me around for a year to see what my life is like not to mention the reality series BS. The answer has always been hell no. Only for y'all and Justice would I even considered it. I'm bringing the biggest producers in the game. I'm not trusting any studio with my reputation. I will allow nothing to impede the IPO launch or hurt my family. The concept and delivery written an executed by Lovie-Belle and you are fine. Make no mistake, Didi, I won't have my legacy tainted. Don't make me regret it." Still chill, but with an undercurrent of hard, cold steel underlying his every word.

"We will do our part, FADE."

She knew that he carefully cultivated his image. She just wasn't so sure that when she finished doing what she needed to do for Justice, he'd be able to manage the fallout.

"Make sure you do."

*J*ust In Case

"Why are you doing this?" Sadiq asked him as they watched from the balcony overlooking the entrance of his home as the two stunningly beautiful women emerged from the limousine.

"Beyond the obvious?" FADE laughed dismissively at his own folly. His eyes never leaving the woman who made his breath catch. He couldn't get her out of his mind after she allowed his touch. He'd not slept without dreaming of her. How she felt. Her touch. She blew his mind. Damn if he'd let her know. She already proved to be reckless with the power she held over him. She made no bones about the fact that the only reason she was dealing with him at all was for the sake of her sister. She blamed him, FADE for — unthinkable and damn near unforgivable on so many levels for Justice's death. That more than anything gutted him. If she thought that then nothing should have compelled her to work with him. And that was why he had to have her close. She was up to something and he need to find out what it was.

"Which one is she? The little curvy one with the hair all over the place?" Sadiq mused, releasing a low whistle showing his appreciation for the view before him.

FADE noticed then how fixated his friend was on the women as they made their way into the house. Delightful was the taller of the two, even in her vans. Lovie-Belle who had obviously caught his friend's attention was laughing at something her sister said, tossing her voluminous curls over her shoulder. She always had trouble taming her tresses, but it only added to her allure. She couldn't have been more beautiful, but his eyes had never been on her but her sister. Her opposite in many ways save her intellect. His sister, Flower and Justice's two sisters had all been extremely smart. Yet, where Flower focused on business, the Howard sisters' interests lie in their writing. A fortuitous choice that so far had earned them their Oscar. He was eager to see what they had to show him. He knew that Lovie-Belle already had an idea and direction. She was not however going to be fodder for Sadiq, who though one of his best and oldest friends was easily out of her league. He would devour her in one bite. He owed Justice too much to allow his sister to be hurt.

"Don't even think about it, Sadiq," he growled. His protective instinct coming forward as he turned to face his friend. "She's not your speed at all."

"Her sister is yours?" he smirked, lifting an aristocratic brow. Being the grandson of a king did nothing to soften his look. He was known for wielding his power and vast resources unapologetically. He answered to no one and FADE was not at all surprised that he did not like being admonished over something he desired.

"That's different. Delightful and I have a history. I gave

their brother my word that I would always look out for them. I haven't gone back on that nor will I. Lovie-Belle is not built for how you get down, Sadiq." FADE knew his friend understood then just how far he would go for Justice's sisters.

"No worries, my friend. I'm here about the work." Sadiq voice was quiet with promise. FADE knew he would keep his word. He nodded, following him down to the living room where they would meet their guests.

SHE KNEW the moment he came in the room. The air instantly became charged. That and Lovie-Belle stopped chattering about nonsense as she often did when she was nervous. Now she was as if she been robbed of speech. Delightful turned from the view of the beach and infinity pool before her and took in the men who'd just sauntered in the room. FADE was in white from head to toe. His shirt open mid-chest showing off his rip cord muscles tucked neatly into his low-slung jeans and all white Chucks. He had on the medallions he always wore a platinum arrowhead with a diamond-encrusted J inlaid. The other on the surface was a smooth arrowhead with no inscription. She'd read they were the first thing he'd bought, and he never took them off. She wondered why one was smooth. Research. Not that she'd stalked his every move through the years or anything like that. The medallion had simply intrigued her the other night. She almost rolled her eyes at herself. Damn, he looked good. Like everything you wanted but knew would make your tummy hurt or in this case pregnant.

"Delightful, Lovie-Belle, let me introduce you to Sadiq Al Rasheed. I'm sure his name precedes him." FADE gave them a wicked smile as Lovie-Belle rushed over to give him a big ol' kid sister hug, which he returned. Her, "I missed you" was muffled but Delightful heard it all the same and felt guilt swamp her until she pushed it down with hardened resolve. There wouldn't be any recriminations until she knew for a fact that FADE had nothing to do with her brother's death.

"I'm pleased to meet you." She tore her eyes away from her hugged up sister to take in the other almost too beautiful man before her. He had tiger eyes and just as tall as FADE's six-foot-two, maybe an inch taller. There was nothing soft about him either. All rip cord muscle bulked out a little more than FADE. Her second thought was that his eyes were cold as fuck and predatory. Ice wouldn't melt in his mouth. A cobra couldn't be more cold-blooded, she thought. The way he assessed her, she had the feeling that he probably thought she was just was mercenary. She was sure FADE had informed him of her play. Good. They both knew with whom they dealt. She allowed a smile to spread across her face. "Please to meet you, Sadiq." He had the nerve to wink as he took her hand, seeming to know she didn't mean it. "Charmed. Utterly." He didn't mean that either.

She laughed, watching as he then turned to FADE and Lovie-Belle. Her breath caught at the coldness of FADE's expression. Or was it barely banked rage? It didn't matter they were here to work. He eased Lovie-Belle away. The dynamic in the room was immediately fraught as she watched her sister's eyes as they rounded like as she came within the thrall of Sadiq. She wanted to shout a warning like they were back to being little and she was about to run out into the street. All she could see was a slow moving wreck and her sister laying under the pile-up that Sadiq would wrought when he crushed her heart. She wanted to grab her hand and pull her away, but it was too late.

"Lovie-Belle, what a fascinating name." Sadiq took her

hand and all Delightful thought as she watched his jaw clench involuntarily was maybe he was not unaffected either.

"You seem fascinated as well, Delightful." FADE stepped in front of her blocking her view of further interaction between the two. She watched his eyes narrow, wondering how he got the words out with his jaw clenched so hard.

"You're getting fascination confused with concern." She huffed, watching as Lovie-Belle and Sadiq moved across the room and began talking about the project.

"You don't have to worry. He's promised to keep it about work." He assured her. His gaze was steady. "I thought for a minute…"

"Boy, please," she laughed, swatting him on his chest. Her breath caught when he caught her hand and kept it pressed against his chest.

"I haven't been a boy for a long time, Didi," he murmured, stepping into her space. "I thought I showed you that the other night. Do you need a reminder?" His tone was low for her but it held a promise.

"You're sure about your friend?" She swallowed against his proximity and the riotous feelings that trilled through her body. The way he held her hand and pressed it against his heart made it hard to question him, hard to look at him without thinking of what he'd done to her body the last time he touched her.

"He keeps his word." He quirked an eyebrow at her bringing her hand up to his lips. When his lips touched the back of her knuckle, kissed then gently bit her she could've come right then. He was a menace.

"Delightful, FADE?" Lovie-Belle called over to them from where she stood before the production board.

FADE let her hand go and walked over to her sister and his friend.

"I'll be with you guys in a second." She headed to the door

leading to where one of the staff said the bathroom was ignoring FADE's smug expression. There was no way she was sitting there for the next few hours feeling squishy.

* * *

"SO WHAT WE really need to do is have a full timeline of events then pick where we'd like to start. A suitable place would be after Justice's passing since that was already been seen in 'Just Us.'" Lovie- Belle was really in her element standing before her white board and story board with her various markers and Flower was proud of her. However, having FADE's movie start after her brother's murder did not fit into Delightful's plans.

"I think to get the full picture of his genius it needs to start earlier." She chimed in, tapping her notes. "His mother said he was a performer at an earlier age. Think back to the Ray Charles movie and What's Love Got To Do With it — both started when they were kids."

"I agree. We need a fuller picture." Sadiq nodded in full mogul mode. From the moment they hit the table, he had been nothing but professional. A cold, calculating professional with straightforward questions and pushing for the best result in every interaction.

"We can do that then go to some school stuff then the deal that launched me." FADE looked up from whatever he was tapping into his phone, then just as quickly returned to the device. Rude. Disinterested. She could strangle him. She knew he was used to always being creative, but this was beyond that. He clearly wanted to control every part of the process. She was one second from telling him he needed to have his sister, Flower, there instead. She knew she shouldn't waste her time because she knew he'd never relinquish that type of control even to someone he trusted more than life.

"Would you rather have Flower cover this part of the process? You know she will have your best interest at heart but is not so close to the story where she can't be objective." She hoped she sounded hopeful and not demanding.

He lifted his head and tilted it toward her slightly. She girded herself for the rage that he barely held leashed. She knew he wanted to call her out about her own actions. He glanced to the others and said instead. "I thought so too to lessen the complications with the project, however, Flower has taken some much-needed time off and is out of the country presently and is taking a sabbatical. She won't be back for the rest of the year."

"FADE," Delightful digesting the fact that he'd not wanted to be part of the project and how that stung. "Okay with love, it makes no sense to skip everything with Justice and you when your whole first album was dedicated to your friendship. We had to skip around a lot in the movie. Your side of the story can only address the origin." She knew she sounded like a schoolteacher reprimanding him but at the moment she couldn't be made to care.

"No." He'd not even looked up.

"The movie won't be the same without what was clearly the key motivator." She pointed to what Lovie-Belle had explained as the catalyst in the character arch.

"No." She didn't think he realized how he grabbed the medallion as he dead-eyed her and went back to tapping into his phone.

"FADE…" She raised her voice, having Sadiq and Lovie-Belle looking between the two of them.

"I thought no meant no these days." He huffed, rising from the table. "Listen, you are going to respect my choice or this ain't happening."

"So you want us to lie?" Delightful challenged him.

"What lies? My past is just that — my past." He leaned in over the table at her. His tone could not be more emphatic.

"People want your origin story. You can even say clamoring for it. You, my man are shrouded in mystery." An unfamiliar voice chimed in from the doorway. Delightful looked up to see who must be Hasan, Sadiq's brother. Twins. It was uncanny but where Sadiq eyes were a golden hazel Hasan's were more greener. Other than that slight difference and Sadiq's hair having more of a curl, they looked nearly the same.

"Brother, welcome." Sadiq smiled, got up and walked over to his brother, kissing him on both cheeks in greeting. "As-Salaam alaikum."

"Wa-Alaikum-Salaam," his brother grinned before turning back to the room. "May I suggest a diversion as until cooler heads prevail?"

"Wassup?" FADE stretched and Delightful could not take her eyes from how his shirt spread revealing the hard plains of his chest.

"We have a premier tonight, so now is the prefect time for a break. We'd love for you guys to join us." He winked at the women.

"Get out!" Lovie-Belle clapped her hands giddy with joy. The only premier they'd been to had been their own. Being indie did not get them the big invitations. This was an excellent opportunity for them. "Aww, that's so sweet you guys but we were only coming for the weekend. We didn't bring outfits suitable for a premier." Lovie-Belle blushed and though brown her skin didn't give her away, her sheepish expression certainly did.

"Never mind that, beautiful. We have that covered." Hasan murmured, striding over to her.

"Don't touch her," Sadiq's cold, clipped words stopped his brother just as he reached for Lovie-Belle's hand, who then turned to give his twin a "Oh, it's like that?" look in return before stepping back. "So how about we get ready for this amazing event?" He rubbed his hands in glee. It seemed to Delightful that Lovie-Belle's excitement contagious.

* * *

DELIGHTFUL KNEW that this was all FADE. The Al Rasheed brothers didn't know them well enough to give them this opportunity. They were FADE's friends. They were doing this at his behest. That was the sweetest, most amazing thing anyone had done for them in this business. Part of her couldn't believe her good fortune having her big brother's best friend look out for them the way he had and the other part of her couldn't trust his motive. Did he want them to be so beholden to him they would look the other way and just forget about Justice?

She couldn't do it. Her purpose was to find out what FADE was hiding. She couldn't hinder Lovie-Belle, though.

"I'm not going Lovie-Belle," she said as her sister stepped out of the bathroom to get ready.

"Why not? We will be in all the entertainment news with the Al Rasheed brothers and people will clamor to know what we are working on and want to give us other opportunities." Lovie-Belle knew and loved the industry. Delightful just wanted to write. She didn't have her sister's same love for all the marketing and PR part of the industry. Lovie-Belle adored it all.

"That's why you need to go. You will knock them dead. Seeing you and FADE with the Sadiq and Hasan will blow up before you even get back here. Your phone will be ringing off the hook from the moment the first photos go viral."

"Ugh. You're right. Help me get ready. You owe me." Lovie-Belle huffed. Delightful knew there was nothing that would have stopped her from going, anyway. She smiled to herself, happy that her sister was getting everything she wanted.

"Be care of Sadiq." She kissed her sister on the cheek after she helped her with her hair. She looked lovely with her massive curls piled high and the mauve Grecian styled gown accenting her curves. The brothers must have had their measurements down to a T. She knew the gown she'd been gifted would have fitted perfectly as well. She was so tempted she couldn't lie. She had to put distance between them. A premier, and the close proximity in a relaxed environment spelled trouble.

"I wasn't the one getting bit," Lovie-Belle quipped as she headed for the door leaving her sister in the center of her bed covering her face with a startled giggle.

CHAPTER 5

*J*ust *Come*

    FADE: What are you doing?

    Didi: Aren't you supposed to be enjoying the premier? How is Lovie-Belle?

FADE: I didn't go.

Didi:….?

FADE: Work. ALWAYS :P

Didi: What Kind?

FADE: Creative Chaos… come here

Didi: Where are you?

FADE: Sadiq's sound studio, lower level.

Didi: 2 work?

FADE: JUST COME

Didi:…

* * *

HE KNEW she never could resist a challenge. Even if it were her just coming down to tell him all caps was uncouth.

"Hey," He looked up only to have his words catch in his

throat. In in her pajamas, she was gorgeous. She had on a pink set with bell sleeves edged with lace butterflies. He smiled to himself, rainbows and butterflies had always been her favorite.

"Hey, yourself." She looked around the studio, taking in the equipment and the wall of windows that looked out on the crashing surf. He loved working in this environment and had done four of his best albums here. Having her here in the space felt magical. Her eyes trained on his fingers as he manipulated the soundboard. "What are you working on?" She asked, seemingly fascinated by the way he manipulated the beat.

"The final song of the movie. Ghadi sent me some sound earlier today." He smiled to himself when he heard her gasp.

"Already?" She turned surprised eyes on him. "How many songs have you created so far?" She sat down in the swivel chair beside him, a stunned look registering on her face. He had seen it many times on producers and executives faces when he presented them with a full playlist within days of their request. What they were in awe of came naturally to him, but it also was his Achilles heel in many ways because when he was consumed with music he could think of little else until his vision was realized. Sometimes he didn't sleep for days and he'd suffered for it. More times than naught, he found it hard to shut his brain off. He had learned to manage his time management better until he received this chance. Since he decided to work with her on this movie, he could do little else than think and breath — her. What she wanted. What she desired. Making her happy was his ultimate goal, it seemed.

"Five."

"Dude, FADE, that's incredible. Are you creating an album to go along with the movie?" Her excitement was contagious.

"Didi…" He shook his head, laughing at her. She'd always been more excited about their music than he and Justice ever were. While they were the most critical of themselves she was their number one fan. Encouraging yet truthful, she gave her often unsolicited advice and praise without reservation. He missed that. With that thought came another darker one.

"So now you give a damn about my music? Is it just for your sister's benefit? Because you want her to have the dopest soundtrack spurring the release?" He watched her head snap back as if he'd struck her. Screw it. She'd been hitting him hard from the moment she sashayed her little ass back in his life making demands and threats.

"Yep." She rocked back in the chair, her eyes cool and assessing. "That's exactly what I want. The way I see it. Two certified hit movies will make my baby sis a force to be reckoned with in this town. There is nothing I won't do to help her fulfill her dream. She wants to be a top director and I want that for her as well." She held up her hands in a 'I don't care' arch and he couldn't have been prouder of her for being no less ruthless than he.

"What about your dreams, Delightful? What do you long for?" He hooked his foot under the ridge of the chair and brought her closer to him.

"I'm a writer. My dreams come true along with Lovie-Belle's. I write, and she directs. No different from you and Ghadi." Her smile was genuine and contagious. He knew in that moment that he would do anything to see her smile like that every day.

"For some reason I don't think you will stop there. I don't see you relenting until you own this town," he laughed, thinking of how ruthless his own sister was. True, he and Ghadi were the creative minds behind their success, but Flower was the power that ran Creative Chaos. His sister, tiny as she was, made music executives quake in their boots.

She was their fiercest advocate. He could see that same drive in Delightful. Nothing would get in the way of what she wanted, and he found that sexy as hell. Despite everything, he wanted to be there when she conquered the world.

"I know you're working on this but if you want to help me flesh out the rest of the story, we can do that as well." She leaned away from him, reaching for the notepads that were ever present so that artists could jot down verses before they entered the booth. Creating music was an organic process. Most of the time music was created in real time over beats or a beat created in the midst of the song.

He closed his eyes against the barrage he knew was coming. He lifted his eyes for her to continue.

"So what do you remember about that time?" She was busy setting up the page like an outline to notice his cringe.

"Excitement." He hummed out a little tune, creating a space in his mind for the emotional toil. "We were just offered this space at the music festival and a tour. We were about to get an agent and manager — the whole nine. You know what it's like to be hungry and on the cusp of that big break."

"Umhm, there's nothing like it. I remember pinching myself. Thinking this can't be real." She looked up, smiling at him. They were caught in that moment. He felt it and he knew she did too.

"There is something else I've never felt again." He whispered, leaning in toward her.

"What was that?" He wondered if she knew how she sounded... How she panted a little. How her pupils widened.

"Kissing you. I've never experienced what I did the first time I kissed you until the other night."

"Really?" She smirked and looked down away from him, unable or unwilling to meet his eyes. It felt like a challenge.

"Yep, and I want that again." He'd like to say that he gave

her plenty of time that he acted a gentleman. Instead, he reached over and plucked her up and put her in his lap. He waited a millisecond for the slap that never came.

When his lips touched hers it was like the first time and the other night. Beautiful, tormented, hot. He felt a surge of heat down to his balls cascading to his dick, lengthening and hardening him to a painful to degree.

"Open for me." He demanded. She did so sweetly. He gripped the nape of her neck with both hands, slanting his mouth over hers. He felt starved. Hell, he was starved. It had only been days, yet he knew he'd been denied what was his, and that made him crave her more. He took her mouth like he owned it. He made her suck on his tongue only to take hers, plundering, urging her on until she whimpered against the onslaught. He nibbled her lips then back at her mouth, pulling her deeper into his kiss. He felt her squirming.

"What do you want Delightful?" He nipped her bottom lip then went to her neck sucking the flesh there into his mouth. Hard. Marking her as his. The darkened purple bruise would be visible to all tomorrow. She clasped him, holding him there. She shifted right on his dick. She pulled away and took his lips this time sucking in his tongue, swirling and nipping him making his dick jump. She knew what she was doing. Pushing him. He would not let her off that easy.

He pulled her back, making her look him in his eyes. "What do you want, Delightful?"

"You," she panted, her eyes pools of need. He could feel her hot little pussy squirming so needily on him. He felt how wet she was too and almost gave in.

"Yeah, baby, I know that. What do you want me to do to you?" He forced himself to ease back and drop his hands loosely at her waist and give her a moment.

"I want you to keep kissing me." She was almost shy about

it. Shy wouldn't do for him tonight. He wanted a woman who knew her own mind.

"Where?" He he lifted his hands and rubbed his thumb over her lips pushing in. Her hot little tongue laving him had his come rising hotly to the tip of his dick. He'd put that mouth to use, he thought, rubbing her lips. "Here?"

"Yes," she whispered, her eyes begging him. He dropped his hand and rubbed the wet, slick digit over her nipples. "Here?"

"Yes," she moaned, arching into his hand. He pinched one as he dropped his head to suck the other hardened tip through her pajama top. He felt her wetness as he sucked her deeper into his mouth. Then lifting his head, he captured her lips again before sliding his hands between her legs, pushing them apart. When he heard her gasp as he pressed his finger against the wet material of her pajama pants. "Here?"

She rode his finger while he held her gaze. He pressed harder. "Do you want me to kiss you here, Didi?" She nodded.

The time for playing games was over.

"Then say it. Tell me, I want you to kiss my pussy, FADE." He growled, moving his hand to rest on her thigh.

She whimpered, and he saw that flash of defiance before she looked him square in the eye.

"I want you to kiss my pussy, FADE."

He turned with her in his lap to the soundboard and pushed up the keys before setting her down on it. "Lift your ass up." He ordered and saw the surprise register on her face a second before she complied. He slid her pajama pants down her legs and placed them under her bottom. Her thighs were silky smooth. He took his time, allowing his gaze to take in the sight that he'd only dreamt about. His breath caught when he finally reached her pussy. It was beautiful. Mine. Was the only word reverberating through this mind as he cupped and massage the plump wet flesh. His to worship. His to ruin.

He eased his chair forward, lifted one leg to start at the ankle. He kissed, nibble and laved her all the way to her inner thigh. He was lost in her scent. His dick was ponding a beat that rivaled his thudding heart, but he was determined to make this the best for her. He moved to the other leg, beginning again. As he reached her thigh, he sucked hard again, and she gripped his head, holding him there. She arched, and he could see just how slick and wet she was for him.

Her clit protruded, beckoning him. He placed a light kiss there. Smiling when she shivered. He squeezed her lips together and took the longest lick up the seam, lapping at the essence of her. He loved how she tasted. He wanted to drown in her sweetness. Every part of her would be his. He took his time laving one side then the other. Spurred by her gasps and moans, he lost himself. Ever a diligent student, he let her guide him in her desire. When she arched, he knew then she was ready for his tongue.

"This pussy is mine," he whispered against her licking inside. Her body answered as she cried out. He pushed her legs apart as he tongue fucked her. Over and over again he licked and laved her. She rose to her hips to meet his every stroke, and he gripped her to bring her closer. His dick pounded as he devoured her. He groaned as her cream came forth. He flicked her clit, lashing her as he moved his fingers to stroke inside.

She rode his fingers and ground herself against his tongue as she came apart for him. Crying out his name, sending shocks of pleasure and torment through his system as he had never felt before. It felt so good and so right to finally be able to give her pleasure like this. To finally have what should have been his all along.

That he'd been denied, rebuffed, and reviled was not lost on him and he felt a pang in his heart as to why.

Easing her legs down, he swiped his face, wiping her essence over his chest. He wanted her so badly, but he could already see this would go like last time and he didn't have it in him to fight for what she should be willing to give him.

He kissed her other thigh, willing his body to calm down. He closed his eyes, hearing her breathing slow as she came back to herself. He couldn't look into her eyes again and see that disdain.

"Are you ok?" He asked, not looking at her. He couldn't. One look and he'd be all over her.

"Yeah." She moved her legs as if to close them.

He sprung from the seat, looking away from her, anywhere but at her.

"Good." Then unable to help himself he glanced, and she was looking up ceiling which just so happened to have a black glass that reflected everything. He saw a myriad of emotions playing across her face and knew he didn't want to wait to see what she decided to settle on.

He barely heard her say, "FADE" as the door closed behind him but kept walking, putting as much distance between them as possible.

*J*ust Incredible

HE DROPPED his head against the marble, letting the hot beads of the water pound down on him in a steady stream. The rush of it making a beat, he absently tapped against the smooth surface. He took deep controlled breaths, moving through the exercises he'd learned from years of therapy, trying to grasp on to his mantra to ground himself. None of that shit worked. Delightful was in every corner of his mind. He could not let her go. He could still taste her after he'd washed every inch of his body. His lust wasn't sated after he'd brought himself to release, thinking of everything she'd let him do. His dick was still ramrod hard. His body wasn't satisfied, and his mind was in turmoil.

Sighing, he shut off the shower and toweled himself off. He moisturized his skin and wrapped a towel around himself. He saw that his phone was lit up. Picking it up, he looked at the message.

Sadiq: We are staying over at my place in Beverly Hills.

He replied with the thumbs-up emoji and tossed the phone back on the bed.

Maybe he could get more work done. Going back to Sadiq's studio was out of the question. He doubted he would ever be in there again without thoughts of her spread open for him as he pleasured her intruding.

He moved to the walk-in closet where he pulled out a pair of sweatpants and grabbed socks and a t-shirt. Walking back, he stopped mid-stride when he heard the tap on the door.

"Yeah," he sounded weary to himself.

"Did you get a message from Sadiq?" Her voice was muffled but there was no way in hell he was opening that door. She was his kryptonite, and he hadn't the strength right now to see her. And of course her concern would be Lovie-Belle. It wasn't like she's be seeking him out on her own accord.

"Yeah," he sighed and rubbed his hands through his wet hair. "It's cool. Sadiq will take excellent care of her."

"That's what I'm afraid of," she laughed, irony dripping from every word. "Are you done running from me, you big ass baby?"

He tossed the clothes on the bed and headed over and ripped the door open. "What do your want, Delightful?"

"Oh, it's Delightful now, huh?" She tilted her head to the side. "I guess it's Delightful once you get what you want."

"And how is it I got what I wanted?" He leaned against the doorjamb, holding his towel in place. He saw how her eyes track him. He saw that she had also showered and changed. More pajamas, another pink set, only this time they were shorts.

"You got your taste but didn't allow me mine," she pouted.

"Then you dipped and left me there, wondering what the hell was going on."

"You had this look on your face like you couldn't decide if you liked the fact I made you come that hard," he ground out. The very thought he had to defend himself to her made anger slither up his spine. "I don't have time for you to figure out if it will upset you every time you let me touch you, Delightful." He stressed her name. That's what she insisted he call her so be it. He'd give her everything she demanded. He had a feeling she be even angrier.

"You know nothing, FADE Snow," she quipped. "Maybe, I thought that was the hardest I ever came, and I was wondering what you'd do next and what you tasted like?"

"Don't." He dipped his head, shaking it back and forth. His control was fraying. Her scent was lifting to him with every inhale. He was salivating with the desire to taste and touch her again.

"Don't what?" She stepped closer. Her body nearly touched his with every rise and fall of her breasts.

"Don't tell me you want that unless you are prepared for me have you in every way I've dreamt for the last twelve years." He reached to touch her cheek, but she turned just in time to kiss his open palm.

"That's exactly what I want, FADE."

ONE MINUTE Delightful was at the threshold of his bedroom door, the next she was in the center of his bed watching as he ripped the towel off his hips. He was flawless. From the top of his head where his hair swirled in disarray, to his corded neck and broad shoulders, his long, ripped torso tapering to an adonis line that had her wanting to dip her tongue in it before she took his dick in her mouth — he was superb. A dick that sprung up from a thick nest of curly hair. So beautiful.

The other night when she took him in hand. She knew he needed double fisting to do the job right, but damn, it would take another set of hands to cover him root to tip. Long, thick, smooth where it needed to be and crowned magnificently. His strong thighs she knew would support her amazing backward's cowgirl move and legs that had no problem carrying her to his bed. He was perfection wrapped up in a tawny package of raw power. And he was hers. If not for the forever he claimed twelves years ago at least for the night.

"Why are you licking your lips like that?" His arrogance made his smile sexy. He'd always had a lovely smile.

"Was I?" She didn't realize she was doing it until that moment. She eased back over to where he stood at the edge of the bed. She crooked her finger, and he came to stand over her with his legs on either side as she sat on the edge. The bed was high, but he was tall so she was almost head level to his waist.

He gasped when she gripped his dick. He moaned when she flicked the tip. She flicked it twice more. "Fuck," he groaned as she slid her lips over the head. It was her turn to moan when he spilled a little, and she lapped him up. He was all tangy deliciousness. She felt her pussy clinch tightly in anticipation. She rubbed her thighs to ease some of the pressure, but it only made it worse. Placing both hands on his hips, she dipped her head deeper, relaxing the muscles in her jaw and throat to accommodate his large size. FADE widened his stance. She took that as a sign to get to work and took him back making him slick and wet adding her hand gliding up and down his shaft.

"Slow the fuck down." He gripped her hair, stilling her. Then pulled her away from him. He stepped back. He was a god standing before her in all his glory. His body was ripped within an inch of its life. He rubbed his hand down his chest over all those hard plains and hefted his dick. "To have this dick is a privilege. Turn around, lie down with your head at the edge," he ordered her.

"Open your mouth." She complied, unable to do anything else under his flinty glare. "Inhale." He was sliding into her mouth. "Exhale." He slid deeper. "Yeah, that's my girl." He held there for a moment. "When I'm done, you're going to still feel me in your throat tomorrow." He pulled out only to return. "That's it, Didi, take my dick down your throat." Sliding out so slowly she could feel every ridge of him across her tongue. She could feel her own wetness pooling between her thighs. She ached. Reaching down, she touched herself. "Hell, yes." He stroked deep into her throat. "Get that pussy ready for me." Grabbing her throat he whispered, "The other night I didn't know if I wanted to fuck you or choke you. Now, I'm going to do both." He eased out until he only rimmed her lips. She kissed and licked him, so far gone on what she was experiencing that it took a moment for his words to register. "Will you let me do that to you Didi? Can I fuck your throat and choke you?" Her eyes searched his, she nodded. He shook his head and loosened his hand. "I need you to ask, FADE, will you please fuck my throat and choke me?"

"FADE, will you fuck my throat and choke me?" She rasped against him. Instinct kicked in when he took her throat. She applied the lesson he'd given. His lips curled as his big hand tightened against her against every thrust. He was careful but no less relentless. The fingers she pressed against her slick folds brought her closer and closer until she was arching into her hand. "You look so sexy," FADE groaned, pushing deeper down her throat. "I knew it would be like this. Your smart ass mouth so hot on me making me come down your throat." Squeezing then releasing only to squeeze again after she'd taken him as deep as she could. "So good," he gritted, stroking into her throat. She took him again and again until she felt him swell as he shouted his release. Her own pleasure overtaking her as she came apart on her fingers.

Delightful saw stars as he pulled her deeper onto the bed before grabbing the towel and tidying them.

"How are you?" He kissed the top of her head. He was still almost as hard as he had been moments before. "I'm fine." She swallowed. He pulled away and looked her for a long moment. Then got up and went over to an alcove that she just noticed had a minibar and poured her some water. When he saw her expression as he returned he chuckled, "Crazy right? You know the Al Rasheed brothers are Moroccan royalty, right? They like their comforts and they make sure their guests have the same. Here." He handed her the glass as he slid in beside her.

"How did you meet them?" She'd been curious about their association, noting in her research that they had been friends almost from the moment they had started Creative Chaos.

FADE sighed, taking the now empty cup and placing it on the bed-side table. He was glorious in his nudity, his long, tumescent phallus swinging with every step he took. "They started out doing videos for me. When they first went into the movie business, their parents weren't pleased and kind of disowned them. I had money, so I seeded them and got some other folks in the music industry to invest. Next thing you know they blew up with hit after hit. Their parents eventually come around and invested in them. Sadiq was the first to suggest we start scoring movies and Hasan introduced us to the right people around tech to help Ghadi see his vision." He shrugged like it wasn't the big deal it was and one of the most amazing things she'd ever heard.

"That's amazing." She looked at him. He was always quietly helping others. Her heart did a dangerous little jig then. She couldn't afford to make this about who he was now. She had to know what he'd done to Justice.

"I wanted you and Lovie-Belle to meet them because I knew they would love you guys and do everything they could to help you out here and look out for you, when I couldn't." He pulled her until she was semi-straddling him.

"You were looking out for us?" She felt her eyes stinging at the sweetness of the gesture. That's something Justice would have done.

"Always." His eyes glittered in the darkened room. He took her lips, groaning when she readily opened for him. She felt consumed by him. He plundered her mouth. Kissing the corners before delving in with his tongue. He kissed her with reverence. Like he adored and treasured her. He was so gentle against her lips. Then kissed her cheeks and eyelids only to come back deeper. Claiming.

"FADE." She pulled back, looking into the golden amber of his eyes. He was biting his bottom lip. She could feel his hardness as it sprung between them. He quirked an eyebrow, waiting for her words. "This between us can't go beyond tonight un-unless you tell me what happened." She sounded rushed. She sounded scared to her own ears.

"You think to give me ultimatums when I'm about to be so deep inside you you won't be able to breathe…" His eyes hardened as he reached over to the nightstand and palmed a foil packet. He said nothing, handing it to her. "Take it. You know you want to. You're just trying to put something else between us. Another barrier. This is the only thing that will be between us tonight. Tomorrow, we'll talk."

Her eyes switched between him and the condom. She took it. Seconds ticked by as Delightful felt her heart racing to catch up with her mind. He'd moved his hands behind his head, resting against the headboard. His jaw was granite, almost in a dare.

Tearing the packet, she removed the slick ribbed material and rubbed it down his impossibly long and hard length.

"Now do what you've been wanting to do from the moment we danced." She cut her eyes at him, giving him her back as she turned and raised to her knees. Grabbing the base, she positioned then repositioned him where he felt best. Slowly she began her decent, taking him inch by delicious inch. Trying as much as she could she didn't think she'd be able to take more of him when she got him halfway. He pulled her back until her back was flush with his chest.

"What about my dick made you think you'd take all of it on the first try?" His whisper was rough and held a touch of meanness as he cupped her in his big hand, massaging her wet flesh as he gave her shallow pumps, easing deeper with each stroke.

"Ahh," she sighed when he drove to the hilt then moved his hands to her breasts. Plumping, squeezing and molding them to his hands. He eased her back up to her original position. She felt so full with him, so hard and pulsing inside. His hands drifted to her back, caressing down and further down until they cupped the mounds of her ass. She felt his dick jerk and swerved her hips, earning her a squeeze as he surged like he couldn't help himself.

"Delightful, fuck me," he gritted. He was holding on by a thread. Ever the diabolical minx, she felt a smile spread over her lips as she swerved again and again, grinding against his hardness. "Ask nicely, FADE. Say Didi, will you please fuck me?" He was so big and deep she knew she wouldn't be able to hold on long.

He gave a pained laugh, "Didi, will you please fuck me?"

Leaning forward slowly, as slow as she could go until only the tip was still inside of her, she glided back down.

Smiling when she saw his toes curl she hit the bottom hard causing him to groan and her to pant.

"Your pussy is so good. So fucking tight. Stop playing. Ride my dick."

She felt herself clinch at his words and her essence spilled forth. He lifted her ass, spreading her further, arching into her downward motions. Her ass slapped against him every time she took him. She ground against him, working her clit between her fingers, fucking him, ruining him. He fucked her back, driving up hard every time she came down. FADE sat up and she felt him hit her spot as he covered her hand with his. He drove deep and deeper still as he flicked his fingers along with hers and they came together. Her essence poured over their fingers as she cried out her release with him groaning hard with his head buried in her neck.

Still holding her he rolled them to their sides before disengaging and disposing of the condom. Coming back, he pulled her close, kissing her neck. His leg was over hers making sure she didn't leave she assumed. He buried his head in her neck again and she felt hot tears choke in her throat.

"I knew it would be like that," he whispered against her skin. "Didn't you?"

She exhaled and nodded. "Always."

CHAPTER 7

$\mathcal{J}$ust The Story

MAD. AS. HELL.

He couldn't believe she'd left his bed last night like some side-chick. He closed his eyes against the bright light of the morning, pulled his sunglasses out of his pocket and put them on as he took his coffee on the southern facing patio of Sadiq's house. This veranda stretched from one end of the house to the other facing the beach, another outside of Sadiq's room also faced the beach, he and Sadiq stood on and looked out the front veranda of the house yesterday that had a view of the hills and one outside of Hasan's bedroom faced the east because he often would do his morning and evening prayers out there.

"Ah, you're awake." Sadiq came and sat beside him with a plate of fruit and his own steaming mug of coffee. "Good morning."

FADE nodded. "Morning."

"Why are you unhappy, my friend? You had a lovely night with your Delightful, so why do you look so mad. Did she refuse you?" He crossed his leg over the other and tilted his head to the side, waiting.

FADE sighed. "She left my bed like a theft in the night."

"I thought we wanted women to leave as to avoid awkwardness?" Sadiq chuckled.

"Not her. This is different," he groused thinking of just how different everything seemed between them as he held her as she slept. Only to wake up to a cold, empty space beside him where she should have been.

"As you have said. Does she know that?" Sadiq quirked an eyebrow at him.

"Yeah." Fade turned back to the horizon not wanting his friend to see the broiling emotions he knew must have been playing all over his face.

"Then maybe it was because she knew her sister would be back early." Sadiq mused as he sipped his own coffee.

FADE shrugged, that was not good enough for him. And he planned on telling her exactly that when he saw her.

"How'd it go last night at the premier?" He changed the subject, wanting to be done with it.

"Excellent."

He almost missed the guarded expression come over Sadiq's face

"And after?' He quirked an eyebrow. He knew Lovie-Belle was lovely and a temptation that few men could resist.

"I kept my word." Sadiq's jaw flexed. "You were on point when you said she was not for me."

FADE nodded, then watched as his friend got up to look out over the ocean.

"Good morning."

The bright sunny words broke in right on the heel of

Sadiq's words. He saw his friend's shoulders stiffen as he turned to greet the newcomers. "Ladies."

He turned then to to see both Delightful and Lovie-Belle take seats opposite him. Lovie-Belle's quick glance to Sadiq was not lost on him. He wondered if she overheard his friend.

"Did you ladies sleep well?" He cooly assessed Delightful, who met his gaze squarely.

"Like a babe," Lovie-Belle said breezily and again. He saw Sadiq stiffen. She didn't seem any worse than when she left, so he decided he'd leave it alone unless he heard different from Delightful.

"Same here," Delightful murmured, taking a sip of an extremely light colored coffee.

"What time are we getting started?" Sadiq turned toward the table, his question directed to Lovie-Belle.

"Ten is fine, unless you need to start earlier?" She smiled at him. The effect seemed to have the opposite on his friend, whom FADE had never seen turn so icily distant before his eyes before. What the hell happened last night?

"I'll inform Hasan and we shall see you then." He nodded then walked away from his own veranda like hell was on his heels.

"Tell us about the premier. I want to hear all about it." Delightful nudged her as she started in on her own breakfast of a bagel and fruit.

As Lovie-Belle regaled them of her newest adventure, FADE sat watching her eat every bite remembering how her lips felt on his. How she tasted every part of him with an enthusiasm that was only matched by his equal ardor.

As they finished the meal FADE stood and reached out to Delightful. "Will you take a walk with me?"

"I'll see you guys at ten." Lovie-Bell giggled as she hurried away.

The only sound that could be heard as they descend the stairs leading to the beach was the seagulls and the waves slapping in the distance.

They walked for a while along the edge of the beach, just missing the water that lapped towards them. It was still early and the sun not shining fully yet. That would change in the next hour our so, but right now the water still held a chill.

"Last night I made you a promise. Today I need one from you." FADE stopped and turned toward her. His heart was beating fast, and he needed to get the words he had to say out fast before they refused to come. He'd not talked about this to anyone ever. Though his family knew they never spoke of the circumstances around Justice's death. The matter had been put behind them. They even looked at him as though he'd done something noble. He didn't know if Delightful would feel that way.

"What is the promise?" Her eyes raked his face, seeming to pick apart every nuance. He knew she was deciding if she would trust him to tell the truth. He didn't blame her but it hurt all the same. And dammit, she should know better.

"What I have to say is between us. No one else can know." His eyes narrowed as her watched her shake her head 'No'.

"My family needs to know. My dad, my mom. Remember them? They were left with no answers. The anguish they felt at Justice's death stills lives with them. It still lives with me too. So if that is what you need you can forget it, buddy.'" She turned away, stalking through the sand like Sofia trumping through the cornfield after Miss Celie.

"Hey!" He rushed behind her grabbing her arm. "I meant no one. I'm sure you want your family to know, Delightful, but this is heavy stuff. Dangerous. You can't say anything."

He could tell by the flash of her eyes that her spirit rebelled at what he was saying. His heart was breaking because he wanted her to know the truth, but how could she keep this truth from her family? Another burden he was placing on her cutting deep into who she was a daughter. He was not playing. This could put his family in jeopardy all over again. He couldn't risk loosing anyone else. He waited, and in the next moment she threw up her hands. "Fine."

"You know how my parents were always really into the community? Well, things got dangerous when the drugs came in. At first it was just a little warning here and there. Soon as they began to make it their business to claim the entire area as part of this one kingpin, Savalle's network then things got really out of hand. They started showing up at my dad's church and driving by our house all times of day and night. My mom kept her advocacy up, encouraging the neighbors to fight back and report on these guys. She was costing them a lot of money. The final straw was her reporting on this one drug house that was using kids as runners. That was a week before everything went down. There was a big raid, lots of folks went to jail. Then Justice was shot. They were really aiming for me. Only the person who pulled the trigger didn't really know us. His reward was they never found his body and left his dog dead in the back of his burned-out car with this guy's chain around his neck. I was the one who was supposed to die that day and I can never tell you how sorry I am that Justice died because of me." He knew tears were rolling down his face and he made a mad sweep to wipe them away. His head fell back as sobs racked his body. He shook with the grief rioting through every pore. It engulfed him as he stood on the beach, the cool sea-breeze ruffling gently through his curls. He gasped as soft, warm arms wrapped high on his waist. Air woodshed put of his lungs on an exhale because she was hugging him so tight.

He pulled back looking down at her head, her hair whipping in the breeze wrapping around his arms. Her own tears running unchecked down her cheeks.

"It wasn't your fault. It was Savalle's fault, that fucking bastard. He did so much harm even after you all moved. That is why my dad was so glad he got a great job so we could move. When he finally went to prison for the rest of his life, that was a blessing." She tucked her head into his chest then.

"He'll never see the light of day." FADE knew the surety of his words. He'd made it so. With his wealth, the least he could do was make sure that his friend's death was not in vain.

"What did you do?" She pulled back and looked at him in awe.

"I made sure that the police had a network of informants to break his network and put his ass away. I was a rap star, what did I care? I was living the high life in New York. They never suspected." His words sounded cold to his own ears. When her eyes lit up, and he knew he'd do it again to make sure she had peace.

"You should have told me," she murmured into his chest.

"I did. You didn't want to have anything to do with me. It was dangerous. I didn't want to put more of a spotlight on your family. Hell, I'd gotten my best friend killed." He pulled back and looked into her eyes. His heart ached with the pain and trust that mingled there. "I was in a bleak place then dealing with my grief then racked with grief and shame. I was in therapy a long time to deal with the trauma."

She stepped on her tiptoes and kissed him with such compassion that his soul soared. Crushing her to him, he knew he never wanted to let her go.

ust the Truth

"WELL, THAT'S DONE." Love-Belle whispered, hugging her close as they hung up with their parents.

"I don't know but that was maybe the hardest thing I ever had to do," Delightful whispered.

"No, it wasn't." Her sister contradicted patting her shoulder. "You told them about Justice."

"Oh, yeah," she mumbled, standing up. "I need to go see FADE."

"So y'all are together now?" Lovie-Belle had a way of lifting her eyebrow in a way that made you feel judged and dared at the same time.

Delightful gave her an eye-roll and grabbed her bag. "Probably never after this. Are you coming back with me or staying here with your new man?"

"He ain't my nothing." Lovie-Belle sneered. "This is business. He and Hasan are the ones who want us to interview and vet the crew. Then we start preproduction midweek. They have met with all of their own people but I also want to give a chance to some of the people who worked on JUST US."

"That sounds good to me. Always have the people who have you." Delightful smiled when she joined her in her brother's lyric.

"All right, give me a hug. I'm sleeping all the way back to Berkeley. Then it's nothing but writing. Sadiq wants this screenplay finished right away." She held out her arms to her sister for a tight squeeze.

"So you're heading out?" FADE's quiet inquiry spoke volumes as she stood in the foyer waiting for the driver came around. His eyes said what he wouldn't. She could sense his longing, and she shared it. But. But. But! How could they possibly go forward? She all but blamed Justice's death on him. Not to mention she'd just done the very opposite of what he'd asked and relayed to her parents everything he'd told her about Justice's death. She didn't trust he'd truly forgive that. Hell, she sure wouldn't.

"Yes." She knew she took the coward's way, looking everywhere but at him. Her resolve to speak the words that would make sure he never spoke to her again burned to ash. She bit the inside of her cheek, forcing the emotions that threatened to spill forth down as far as she could push them. Guilt racked her. Fear raced across her spine like a careening chariot. What she'd done was unforgivable, but she couldn't say she wouldn't do it again. Her parents finally had some sense of closure. They were owed that. The rest she'd deal with in good time.

"I have to go check-in with Creative Chaos because Ghadi

is holding everything down by himself now that Flower is on sabbatical." He stepped toward her and grasped her chin, tilting her head up so she had no other choice but to face him. "After that I'd like to come see you. Will you let me do that, Didi?"

She swallowed. What they'd shared the other night. Then on the beach. He'd come to her baring his soul. Could she turn him away? Her heart squeezed. Was this real? She'd spent so much time running from him. Was it even possible for them to forge a future? Not likely after what she'd done…

"FADE…" She stepped back, shaking her head slightly. He followed her. She was pressed against the door. There was a hairbreadth between them, but his arms hung loose at his sides.

"Don't do this, Delightful," he gritted. "Stop. Fucking. Running." His eyes blazed with want.

The door pressed open, pushing her slightly into him. He pulled her close.

"Miss Howard, are you ready?" The driver asked, picking up her bags.

"Yes, I'll be there in a moment." She smiled at the man before she turned to finally face the one before her.

"Okay." She looked into his eyes. "I am going to be super busy writing the screenplay."

"Well, it's good that you will have its subject on hand in case you get stuck won't it?" He smiled and pulled her to him, taking her lips. She closed her eyes to allow herself this one thing, basking in the adoration with which he claimed her. Lost. In. Him. His lips were everything girls wished and hoped for. His tongue delved, captured, and claimed her down to her soul.

He swung his arm around her shoulders. Kissing her neck before he tucked her into the car.

Relaxing back into the cool confines of the town car, she daydreamed about that kiss between her two naps on the way home.

DELIGHTFUL GOT UP TO STRETCH. It had been a solid four hours since she'd had a break, but she could say she was pretty much done. The words had flowed from her like fire after the weekend she'd had. Her entire world was FADE at the moment. Everything she'd experienced with him last weekend had gone into the screenplay she'd crafted and after the feedback she'd gotten from the Al Rasheed's production team including Lovie-Belle, who'd somehow finagled a producer credit, she was totally pumped feeling like she was on the top of the world. She had to admit her work had improved since JUST US, whether it was maturity growing as a writer or FADE as her inspiration the final result was something she could hold her head up with pride and present to the Academy again.

She knew there needed to be tightening around some of the dialog. She'd caught the essence of FADE, his soul spoke to her so how could she not? Lovie-Belle told her of the promising unknown actor they'd found to play young FADE and the after seeing his pictures she knew that this guy, Chisom was something special. They all thought he'd be prefect for the part.

Walking over to the desk she never used, she picked up her phone looking at the overwhelming number of calls she'd gotten since she'd sat down for her second writing session for the day. Her brow crinkled, there'd been none earlier. She'd silenced her phone as she normally did when she got to this little getaway cottaged she rented whenever she had a deadline. This was her spot. Lovie-Belle was back, and she was just noisy. She couldn't help it. She just was. When Delightful needed to really buckle down, she had decided to come out to this little bungalow near Tilden State Park to get her work done. If she were lucky she'd get reimbursed by the studio. If not, she'd claim it on her taxes. There was nothing cheap about the upfront cost of being a writer regardless of the genre or format one wrote.

Her phone began buzzing as soon as she turned it on. It was one of her many cousin's from Birmingham, Kaia.

"Hey," she said, not bothering with any preliminaries.

"Delightful? Girl, have you seen all this stuff about FADE being a snitch all over the blogs? Well, it did not come from any of us just FYI! I know how you hold a grudge and nobody wants you mad with them." She nervously rushed through everything so fast it took a moment for the news to register.

"What are you talking about?" A dead weight settled deep in the pit of her stomach. The FUCK. She quickly scrolled through the texts and calls on her phone.

"It had to be one of the other Loves. You know their country asses can't hold nothing," Kaia huffed. Yes, everyone called her a grudge holder because she'd cut FADE out of her life. Family loyalty had made a great many of her kinfolks do the same. Some may have even leaked the story she'd told her mother, which she said not to share by the way, to exact some type of retribution. She should have known her mother would not keep this just to her and daddy. Kicking her own ass mentally as dread flowed like acid in her veins, her mind scrambled and immediately lit on FADE.

"Kaia, thanks for the heads up. I have to go." She hung up before her cousin could launch into anything more. This was a mess of her own making.

She covered her forehead and close her eyes. Scrolling

back through messages until she came to the top. Her heart had stopped looking at a message from several hours ago.

FADE: I'm boarding the jet.

Then

FADE: I can't believe you.

She looked at her phone then and she had over a dozen missed calls from him and half that many from Lovie-Bell with one message saying for her to call as soon as she took her break. She was taking her break but there was no way she could call anyone with this being the result.

Scrolling back through the messages, she tapped on more of her sister's later messages.

LB: OMG. FADE is here… What should I say?

LB:???

LB: I told him you only told mom and dad.

LB: He wants to know where you are. Do you want me to tell him?

JUST THEN HER phone buzzed again. She closed her eyes. She knew her sister wouldn't tell him unless she said it was okay. She turned off her phone. What could she say? She told her parents. They told the rest of the family. It was that simple. He'd asked her not to. She felt her parents should know. She pushed him. There was nothing for it.

Like a robot, she splashed water on her face. The only thing she could do was move forward with the screenplay and pray that he didn't ask for her to be replaced as the writer and Lovie-Belle as director. This was a primary breech of the Nondisclosure Agreement they'd signed, not to mention the moral clause that the Al Rasheed's insisted on.

She could count her career over after it was found out that one of her knuckled-headed extended family members was the thumb-thug behind this viral attack on FADE's reputation and integrity. Street cred gone. Name mush. There was no coming back from a slur of being a fucking snitch, not ever in the rap game. Deuces.

She didn't know how long she sat there staring at her now blank screen. Shaking herself, she sent a quick email to her sister along with the final draft of the screenplay. Maybe they could salvage something.

She got a glass and poured some Sofia Rose' and sat back on the little bungalow couch. There wouldn't be any more work tonight, maybe never. She should have left well enough alone. She should have told FADE when she had the chance that she'd told her parents. Now that it was out they probably were in danger even if her big mammoth of a cousin, Rafe-Leroi, who was part of the elite CRU, like SWAT but tougher lived in the city with his six sisters and could protect them if need be.

The knock almost sent her flying off the couch. Her heart was beating like it wanted to jump out her chest. She looked at her clock on the wall over the tiny fireplace. It was past midnight. No one should be here at this time. This wasn't even the prime season for people to visit the national park.

She debated commando crawling over to the kitchen and getting a butcher knife. The wood door shook under two hard thumps.

"Delightful, open the door."

Her breath stuttered. It was definitely FADE. There was no mistaking his voice, though muffled through the door. Two more hard thuds. Her eyes darted around even though she knew she had nowhere to go.

"Delightful."

There was so much expectation behind those words.

There would be a reckoning, he promised with every syllable uttered. She tripped over to the door. She wasn't tipsy, just nervous. She'd have words with Lovie-Belle before she strangled her. To her credit, she thought of FADE as a brother and thought he would do nothing to harm her. She hadn't heard the cold clarity of how he'd spoken, of how he'd handled reprisal for Justice's death. She knew he left things out about how he'd handled the situation. He didn't have to say she knew how men like FADE operated in this world. They got shit done. Period. They rarely let people slide on a slight, let alone the type of betrayal he now knew her capable.

She noticed the way her fingers trembled as she turned the locks. She jumped back as the door flew in front of her and banged loudly against the wall. The flimsy doorstopper was nothing compared to the force of him thrusting open the door.

He turned to close the door and locked it with a decisive snick of both of the locks.

Facing her, his face florid with rage, he walked her back to the wall in front of the door. She felt her hair snag on the wood. He slapped his hands on the rough panel, preventing her from moving an inch.

"I fucking trusted you, Delightful. I told you how serious this was. Then what? You go to these trash-ass wannabe news outlets about me?" He ground out, his face inches from hers.

She winced shaking her head a huge piece snagged, but that alone wasn't why she felt tears smart her eyes.

"No. No, I'd never do that. I'll give you my computer, and phone, you can have your IT people do a search. I wouldn't. I know how much it meant to you."

"You knew how much it meant to me and still you ran your mouth? You want me to believe you didn't leak it? Then who did you tell?"

"M-my parents. Look, I told you they had to know."

"You made me a promise," then he laughed bitterly. Ugly. Shook his head and stepped back and turned back to the door. "Yeah, another fucking promise."

"FADE, wait." Reaching back, she tried to untangle herself enough to follow.

"What are you doing?" He stopped and frowned, watching her struggle to get free.

"My hair is stuck in this panel," she muttered, trying to no avail to detach herself.

"Be still." He walked back over and looked behind her. "A fucking mess. Ease up on your tiptoes." She did with a promise to herself she'd keep her hair tied up after this. Nobody had time for this. Her eyes rounded when he took out a Gerber pocket knife and before she could say, STOP, he snipped the hair lodged in the crevice. A full two inch lock of a snarled curl forlornly hang out of the wall.

"You did that on purpose." She rounded on him.

"So did you. Do you know what you've cost me with this little stunt of yours? My WHOLE FUCKING CAREER. Everything Ghadi, Flower and I have worked our asses off is probably gone. Did you think of them at all in your petty plot to crush me? The movie is dead. No one is going to come see a movie about a sellout ass rapper. You fucked me and then you really fucked me over. For what?" His voice was hoarse with desolation. She could feel it in the very air she breathed.

"I'm so sorry, FADE. Let me explain." She let her hands hang at her side. She'd not been around him long and never heard rumors of him being violent, but if there was a cause to be, it was now. She stepped away from him into the living room but not letting her eyes stray away from him.

"So you fear me now?" His face hardened so much that he could give the bronze statue of Dr. King in Kelly Ingram Park back home a run for its money.

"You, destroyer of everything good, have got to be kidding me," he scoffed. Taking the path opposite her to come around to sit in the recliner opposite the couch. It swiveled so it could face the fireplace to its right. That and a table was as much furniture as the small cottage allowed. There was an eat-in kitchen where she sometimes worked. Then one bed with an ensuite bath.

She took her place back on the sofa and faced him. "My parents needed to know. They'd gone all this time not knowing what happened or why. The police were not that forthcoming. Now we know why. They were protecting your family. I get it. Now they can have closure." She clasped her hands in front of her, pleading with him to understand.

"That sounds so perfect and your motives to pure but you've forgotten that you stood out on that beach and said you wouldn't do that. I should have known, but it is obvious that your word means nothing to you nor do I. You knew when I walked you back to the house you would tell your parents." He was gripping the leather so tight it squeaked. She hoped he wasn't wishing it was her neck.

"I do care about you." She slid forward, catching his hand. "I'm sorry I went about this all wrong." She swallowed back tears. She knew she had no right to them and would not weaponize them against him to use to her advantage in this situation she'd brought on herself. "I was wrong. I broke your trust. I wanted to tell you before I left. I put it off once you asked if you could visit. I thought you'd be too mad then you'd be done with me before I had a chance to explain. Before we had a chance..." She bit her lip, turning away from what look like hatred rolling off him in waves.

"A chance at what?" No emotion, only icy disdain greeted her when she turned back to face his amber eyes that had once burned so hot for her. Now they looked like a Siberian tundra.

"To be together," she whispered.

He was slow to blink. He turned his face away from her so she saw his chiseled jaw working. When he once again met her gaze his eyes were ablaze with amber heat.

"Show me."

CHAPTER 9

 *ust Beg*

"Stand up." The command burned through the air like a California brush fire. Inside, she knew this was not making up for her actions. They were unforgivable. She didn't expect his forgiveness. She maybe didn't even deserve it. He wanted her that was more than clear with his spread legs not hiding anything. She stood.

"Take your clothes off." She didn't hesitate, only stripped out of her pajamas which she'd long ago found were the most comfortable thing for her to write in. She kicked them aside.

"Come here." She took one step, then he raised his hand.

"Is that how you show contrition?" His eyes narrowed as he watched her kneel, then beckoned her forth. She'd heard it whispered he had Dom tendencies. She was so wet she could feel her essence slicking her thighs.

When she reached his sprawled legs, she knelt like a good girl awaiting her next instruction.

"Take me out."

Rising, she unbuckled, unzipped and gently maneuvered him out of his jeans. His dick stood, long and hard in all of its magnificent glory with just enough curve encased in smooth skin to keep it interesting and it was already pearled. She licked her lips and leaned forward. His hand snaked out like a viper and fisted her hair, stopping her cold. "You forget yourself," he chided, menace dripping from every word.

Silence beat between them until she realized what he wanted.

"FADE, may I taste you?" Like magic, his hand loosened just enough for her to take him in her mouth. His breath whooshed out in a rush as his thighs flexed under her hands as she used them for leverage. The angle was tricky as she tried to take as much as she could the way he'd showed her he liked. She had a little less than a third on her descent. He was just too dang big. Too hard. She snuck a peek at him underneath her lashes, seeing how he watched her every movement. Their eyes met. She knew her eyes were as soft as his were hard. Ever so slowly, she eased up until only the tip remained. She swirled his tip. Over and over again her glided her tongue over him before sliding down one side then the other and lower until she sucked his sac deep into her mouth and rolled him around her tongue.

His breath caught as he tried to hold himself still. His back arched anyway. Their eyes locked again. His jaw ticked. She released him, came around the side and draped herself over the arm of the chair. He held her by the small of her back to steady her as she took him in deep long sweeps to the back of her throat. Pleasure and a tightening pain closed around her throat as he surged up to meet her every stroke. She fucked him with her mouth and he groaned every time he hit the back of her throat. Again and again she took him. His hips pumped hard. He gripped her bottom, smearing her wetness all over her arching ass. "Didi," he gasped as he shot ropes of come down her throat.

She slipped back to the floor at his knees. Waiting. Would he leave? There was no doubt that he was still livid. Watching him, she saw the shadows under his eyes and the sheer fatigue. She knew he'd been on his way to see her but he looked like he'd not had a good rest since they'd left Malibu.

She almost fell back when he stood. His jeans hung low on his hips. He pulled her to her feet. His gaze was cynical and troubled. He was fighting himself. She hesitated to speak. She didn't want to sway him in any way. Her heart longed to comfort him, but she knew that was the last thing he wanted from her at the moment.

His eyes searched hers. She hid nothing. He sighed, his head hung forward for a moment. "FADE," she gasped startled as he threw her over his shoulder holding her steady by her ass as he strode from the living room.

* * *

WHAT THE FUCK are you doing, man? He thought to himself as he lay Delightful down on the queen-size bed, unable to tear his gaze away from her hot little body. He should have left. Hell, he never should have come, but he had to hear it from her own lips how she betrayed him. He had so much to do before his charity event. Which would not be canceled no matter what was going on in his life. The people of Shelby-Love, Alabama needed his and Creative Chaos support. They'd finished a plant where they made the chips for all their devices three years ago. They'd built two libraries and a health clinic. A youth center and a veteran center were recently built, and he was going there for the dedication and celebrations that followed.

Part of him coming to Berkeley was to ask her to accompany him there. Hoping this would be the first of many events they attended as a couple. Now that dream was deferred. But this he decided was not out of the question. He would get her out of his system once and for all and be done with this whole fucking mess. Some dreams you just had to give up on.

She spread her legs, and he knelt before her like angels were calling him home. He wanted to worship her pussy and punish it simultaneously. And he would. He slid a finger inside of her as he captured her hardened little nub in his mouth. Sucking and swirling his tongue over her. Her taste was intoxicating. His second finger joined the first. Slowly he fucked her drawing out her want, retreating to barely there flicks and licks when she was close. A soft sheen of perspiration lit upon her body, making her shimmer. She arched, thrashed, her legs scissored as he brought her closer and closer only to retreat.

Sitting back on his hunches his gaze tracked from her weeping slit, past slick tone legs, to plump thighs, her tummy that was sucked tight in anticipation of what he'd do next, her rising and falling chest and full breasts, her nipples high and tight beckoning, begging for him.

"Is there something you need, baby?" he whispered. He smiled, watching her arch against his fingers as he ran light trails of her essence over her nether lips and smeared it over her clit.

"Yes." Her voice was plaintive. "Please let me come, FADE."

"Good girl," he groaned against her as he thrust two fingers in her before ruthlessly sucking the mound of her pussy into his mouth capturing everything she had to give him in strong hard pulls. Then he pulled back and fucked her in tandem with flicks and swirls of his tongue. He pressed her G-spot and flicked her clit.

"FADE," she cried his name as he made her come hard against his fingers and mouth with her essence drenching his hand and face.

"Turn over." He growled, his dick slapping against his stomach after he shucked the rest of his clothes. He came to the edge of the bed and crooked a finger.

"Head down, ass up," he instructed. He saw her hesitation even as she did what he commanded.

"I've never…"

He looked at her tight rosette and felt himself hardened to an almost painful degree.

"I'd never ask you do anything you weren't comfortable with. It's your hot little pussy I want." He eased the condom down his straining erection. He wanted to roar with triumph and agony when she rested her head on her folded hands and spread her knees apart to accommodate him. She was dripping for him. He nudged her apart and slid in. She gasped. He groaned. She was so fucking tight, even in this more accessible position. Sweat broke out on his forehead.

"You feel so good, Delightful. I could almost forget…" his words of praise trailed off, and he was lost in the overwhelming sensations of his dick going deeper, as deep as she could take him in spearing increments.

"I don't want you to forget," her breath caught on his thrust. He felt a rush of her essence. And thrust again. She was so close. He stilled. "Don't you fucking come yet, Didi."

"I'm trying not to, FADE, but I don't know if I can stop. You feel so good, baby. Let me come on your dick, please," she pleaded and pushed herself back, impaling herself on him again and again like she couldn't help herself. He matched her thrust with his own.

"I like the way you beg for my dick, Didi." He thrust shallow then deeper, feeling his own climax approaching unable to resist the sweet pull of her body.

Gripping her hips, he steadied himself, bracing one foot on the floor and raising the other beside her thigh.

"Let me know if it's too much." He whispered, lengthening his downward stroke.

"OhMyGod, FADE," she cried out, looking over her shoulder, her gaze pleading, and his thrust became relentless. Over and over again he pile drove to the hilt. His body smacking into her. He watched as her ass shook. He reached around stroked her clit in light relentless flicks. "FADE." Her luscious grip on his dick tightened, making his toes curl. She was heaven. He gave her no quarter, each thrust as hard as the last. He watched as she bit her arm, stifling her cries of pleasure as bliss took over. Seeing her, feeling her come so hard for him sent him spiraling toward ecstasy, his own release nearly making his knees buckle.

* * *

HER EYES WERE cruddy when she peeked. The pink dawn was just barely there, but that wasn't what woke her. It was the cool, empty space beside her. He was leaving. She'd felt the dip in the bed but assumed he'd just went to the restroom, barely registering his movement. He didn't return, and he'd gotten his clothes.

She sat up, calling herself ten times a fool. She grabbed her wrap before heading out to the front room.

"You're leaving." A statement because it was obvious he was as she watched him pull on his sneakers.

"Yeah." He tied the last shoe and stood.

He was like a ghost — already gone. So far removed from her he may as well be on the other side. There was no way she could ever reach him now. She knew she had no right. She knew what last night was. A good bye. But still. But. Fucking. Still. Anger rose within her despite the reality she was faced with as she watched him head to the door.

"Without saying anything, like a coward?" She challenged following him.

He stopped and turned so suddenly and turned that she ran right into his chest. He stepped back as if scorched. Then leaned in, tilting his head low, his eyes cold amber orbs and his mouth curving into a cruel smile. "I gave you the best goodbye of your life, Delightful."

Her hands curled into fists and her nails bit into her flesh, tears smarted. "So much for all that wanting me for twelves years. The first moment something happens, you bail."

She watched in horror as his hands reached out. Her breath stuttered as he cupped her face. The achingly soft caress broke her. Tears pooled, then spilled over his thumbs. He touched his forehead to hers. "That something was you, Delightful." Then his lips touched hers in a gentle, angel's breath of a kiss.

"Goodbye, Didi."

She could not fathom how she remained standing as he turned and walked away or not ran pleading with him to stay, perhaps the finality of his words. It wasn't until she heard the car pull away did she crumble where she stood and felt grief like she had only one other time in her life.

CHAPTER 10

J ust Survive Somehow

"WE HAVE a fantastic turn out today too, nephew." FADE despite feeling like his heart had been scraped out by a rusty spoon smiled at his aunt, Mattie-May. She could not or would not for any reason call him by anything other than nephew or Fernando, which was also his dad's name, so that became bothersome to her when they were all together. She didn't hold with rap music or hip hop no matter what he, Ghadi or Flower had done for the family or her community of Shelby-Love, Alabama. Nope. Only gospel music, which was all he'd heard since he'd got into town yesterday for the openings of the youth center yesterday and veteran's center. Not that he minded. He like gospel, even the old school mass choir joints. He was sure she was trying to save him from the world. She didn't want to hear anything about what he did for a living if it had nothing to do with his faith. It would take Ghadi, who was way less diplomatic about the issue, to point out how the very same people with square jobs were the ones getting into the most shenanigans. He'd rather not argue, just come every year and give back the best way he could with genuine opportunities to the small rural community that had only one industry before he, Flower and Ghadi decided to place their tech company here instead of overseas. Now Shelby-Love had two major industries that hired more than half the community. Shelby Sugar and the now the Creative Chaos tech factory that created chips and smart devices for everything you could imagine from toys, cinema and NASA.

"Well, I'm glad to hear it. I'm sorry Marchellis couldn't make it. He had an engagement in Japan that he couldn't reschedule. I know having the hometown son would've meant a lot to these guys." He smiled over at her as the town car headed up the hill to the event. He saw that she was not kidding about the turnout. There had to be at least five hundred people there. He knew from his conversations with Marchellis that a huge number of vets lived in this area with needs that were vast. Creating a veteran's center where they could received not only outreach but real monetary help was essential to the area so people would have to travel the almost hundred miles to Birmingham.

He snapped a pic and sent it to his friend, though he knew he'd probably not see it for hours because of the time difference. It surprised him when he got a quick reply.

MARC: That's what's up!!! BTW I need to hit you up when I get back.

FADE: Will do. *Thumbs -up*

. . .

POCKETING his phone he turned his attention back to the gigantic crowd at least for this area that awaited. This was amazing. They would do a lot of good here. Part of the issue with outreach was reaching people who wanted to go through with the process in this case if they needed therapy. He knew firsthand how integral getting therapy for PTSD could help you live with it and not drown in depression.

The town car pulled up alongside the dais. There was an enormous bow held by ribbons. The mayor, Connor Love, was there along with Dr. Matthias Shelby, a former green beret and hometown hero turn trauma surgeon would head the clinic. They'd lined his security team up alongside both sides of the stairwell. They were unnecessary in his opinion, but Flower would have a fit as would his insurance company if he'd said no.

He stepped out to a wave of cheers and clapping. He helped Mattie-May out of the car and handed her over to one of his security detail as she went to take her place at on the front row. He waved to the people and rushed up the stairs.

"Hey Y'all! Thank you for coming out to the grand-opening to the Carrington Veteran's Center. As you know my father, Rev. Fernando Carrington served in the army and has dedicated his life to being of service to his fellow service members. Though he can't be here today, this happened because of him. So, when you see him the next time he's in town, make sure you shake his hand or offer him a cool glass of lemonade or sweet tea! Now let's get this place opened so we can help some folks and eat. My aunt Mattie-May made her famous peach cobbler." He laughed as the crowd's unrestrained cheering. He loved this place. The south would always be home and Shelby-Love was the place both he and Delightful's parents hailed. That was why this day was so bittersweet.

Pushing those thoughts away to deal with later, he turned to shake the mayor's hand and take the oversized scissors he'd use to cut the ribbon of the veteran's center. He saw a movement in his peripheral vision. He saw a glint of shiny blackness, a flash, then another and another before blinding pain exploded and everything went black.

* * *

"BREAKING NEWS" the news crawled across the screen. What followed made Delightful scream and scream.

"Delightful, what?" Lovie-Belle rushed into the room and stopped short at the words of the reporter. Delightful barely registered her sister's matching cry of horror, too busy listening to the rest of the news rocketing the airwaves. "Rap star and business mogul Fernando Anthony Duke Ellington Carrington known as FADE what shot at a two-day charity event last evening in Shelby-Love, Alabama and medivacked to the UAB trauma center in Birmingham, Alabama. There is a news conference scheduled for later today." She listened as the newscasters went on to speculate at the reasons why the shooter chose FADE and his possible connection to the Savalle syndicate.

"This is my fault," she whispered, helpless to do anything other than watch as the newscasters and pundits picked apart FADE's life like he was a common criminal instead of a victim of a violent crime. Then they went into how rap and hip-hop was a stain on the culture.

"I have to go see him." She rose from the sofa where she had somehow found herself.

"Do you think that is a good idea? You said he left you at the cottage like he never wanted to see you again." Lovie-Belle's words though spoken in the softest tone eviscerated her.

"I know," she sobbed. "But I can't not go see him." She strode to her room and closed the door. Walking over to her closet she grabbed a bag tossed in a pair of jeans, a couple of t-shirts, her bonnet and tooth brush. She called an Uber and texted hr cousins to let them to know she'd be staying with them a few days.

"Hey," she said walking back into the living room, "My ride will be here in a sec."

"Good." Lovie-Belle put her phone down and stood in front of the couch. "Sadiq just texted to reschedule our meeting this week. He and Hasan are on their way to Birmingham and said that you could fly with them."

Delightful closed her eyes in both relief and dread. She'd not talked to either man since the fallout over the leak. They only emailed saying that their production team, Creative Chaos, and the studio were handling the PR and she was to have no further contact with the media unless explicitly allowed to by the team. She didn't bother explaining her side. She only gave them all her devices so they could do a forensic search to verify that she had not released the information herself. She was well aware that she was hanging on by a very thin thread.

Her phone binged, letting her know ride was there.

"I love you, I'll call you when we land."

"I love you back." Lovie-Belle hugged her back, "I'm going to keep both of y'all lifted."

"Thank you, sugar," she whispered into her neck.

"When you get the chance, Delightful. You need to tell him you love him." Lovie-Belle pulled back, looking at her steadily.

"I will." She ducked her head under the intense scrutiny of her sister's gaze, got her bag and went out to the waiting car.

ust Live

"WE'RE HERE." She started at Sadiq's gentle touch.

"Ok." She stood. She couldn't believe she'd actually slept. She'd been exhausted, and for most of the flight she sat looking out of the window. The Al Rasheed brothers and been kind and had not even admonished her in the least. They'd taken one look at her, she thought, and decided to give her a break. She knew she looked a mess and a half.

"Is it possible for me to freshen up?" She asked, standing before him.

"Sure," He nodded toward the rear of the jet.

Smiling, she stepped past him and made her way to the restroom.

"Jeeze," she muttered, looking at the shadows and hollow look on her face. Haggard should have her face beside it in the dictionary. She hurried through her ablutions and pulled her curls up in her favorite pineapple style, keeping her hair out of her face and safe from tangles. She was still a sight, but she at least wouldn't scare small children looking like some witch ready to snatch and eat them. She headed back out to the somber men waiting for her at the front of the plane.

"Any word?" She asked as she approached them.

"Ghadi said he'd fill us in when we got there." Hasan answered, indicating that she should proceed them out of the plane.

Whatever she wanted to ask melted away when she debarked and looked out at the beautiful city that was her home. She'd missed it and had not found her way back to it very often even though her parents live in a quiet superb of the city. The fact was she could not set foot in her home state without thinking of her brother, how much she loved him and how he should be here. She loved him with everything and his loss left a hole so deep she never thought she'd be able to fill it.

She inhaled, taking the sweet honeysuckle scent that permeated the air. Her chest tightened, and tears filled her eyes. Swiping the wetness away, she finally admitted to herself that the time she'd spent with FADE had been the most content she'd been since Justice's death. He had been the piece that was missing. She knew that she would never be able to redeem what she'd done, but he would know that she cared enough to come.

* * *

THE RIDE to the hospital was quick, the city lights passing them by in a blur. They barely spoke the entire trip, all of them lost in their own world. Sadiq was busy texting and working from his phone and when he spoke after a quick apology to her he relayed information to his brother in

Arabic. She didn't mind consumed with her own thoughts and memories until they pulled into the parking deck of the hospital.

From there the hospital officials and security escorted them into the building and to what was clearly marked the Intensive Care Unit. Her throat contracted, and she was grateful she didn't eat the food Hasan offered her otherwise it would've erupted out of her mouth then. Justice never made it to the hospital. Not this level. Her parents had not let her come to the morgue to identify him. Walking down the hall leading to the private suite they'd set aside for FADE, Delightful couldn't help but notice the somber atmosphere. The air was thick with tension and fear. Maybe it was just this entire floor because most of the people were so critically ill. She hoped it had nothing to do with FADE.

Rounding the corner, they came up on the suite and there were maybe twenty people, many of his family. Her steps faltered. Looking at the faces of his family who gathered. What was she thinking of coming here? They were clustered in separate groups. She saw that Ghadi, Willow and FADE's parents all huddled together talking to a doctor. Mrs. Carrington looked to be sobbing, and Delightful's heart twisted viciously.

She must have made some sort of sound because every head swiveled their way. Stepping away from his cluster, Ghadi moved in her direction, his face etched in fury. His long wiry form bristled, and she got the feeling his strike would be as quick and deadly as a viper.

He stopped short, looking down at his arm. His mother held his arm and shook her head slightly as if to say this was not the place. Delightful understood, who knew who'd tell the story of their confrontation to the tabloids and blogs.

She sighed, thankful for the momentary reprieve. She held his gaze. She would not shy away from his ire. Hell, she welcomed it. As long as she could see how FADE was doing. She watched as FADE's mom came toward them.

"Sadiq, Hasan, thank y'all for coming to check on my baby." She smiled sadly at them. Pulling them each into a hug. When she turned to face her, Delightful wanted to run in the opposite direction. Then soft, warm arms warped around her. "Delightful, honey. We've missed you, especially FADE. Don't stay away this time."

"I'm so sorry," she whispered on a sob as FADE's mom just held her. She squeezed her eyes closed against the emotion that shook her body.

She didn't know how long she stood there before the words registered, "Shh, it's ok. He's going to be fine. He will need extensive therapy and they've already replaced his kneecap with cadaver tissue but say it will be like new. One of the bullets cut through his leg so it needed titanium pins. He's made it through the roughest part. They also got the guy who attacked him. One of the guys there was a former green beret, and he took him out right there." She hugged and patted Delightful. "No more tears now."

"Mrs. Carrington..." She stopped at the raised hand.

"Grace."

"Grace, I'm sorry for everything. You looked so upset when we walked up that I feared the worse." Delightful saw that the troubled look returned to the woman's face and could kick herself. She had to know everything.

"We were talking to the doctor taking care of Flower. She got very sick yesterday when she arrived from Japan. She's out of the woods now, but she'll also have to recover from her ordeal."

"Oh, that's terrible." Delightful hugged her knowing how much she loved her kids. So much hardship being visited on them. "Flower is such a light and always so kind."

"We don't know everything. We hope when she awakes she'll tell us…"

"Mom." They both looked up to see Ghadi towering over them. She saw the Al Rasheed brothers were back in the waiting area talking to Willow, FADE's younger sister and Marchellis. Ghadi had made sure that only she remained outside.

"Dr. Ahmad is ready to take you and dad to see Flower." His words were gentle to his mother, but his eyes were on her.

"They brought snacks if you are hungry, honey. I know you had a long trip." Grace gave her arm a quick squeeze and patted her second son's arm before walking toward her husband and the doctor. As she watched Grace leave with the doctor, she knew what was going to follow.

"Ghadi, I just wanted to know if he was okay." She may as well have been talking to a wall.

"You mean after you almost got him killed?" He kept his voice low. He was taller than FADE, so he towered over her. Wiry and rippling with hostility. There was no mistaking his anger. It rolled off him in waves. She felt the full brunt of his hatred. He did not try to hide how he felt. She knew she deserved it. She faced him unflinching. "I know what I did. FADE knew and why. What you are feeling for him right now take that and magnify it a hundredfold. Then you know how I feel. That doesn't make me telling my parents what really happened to Justice right, but just like you want answers about what happened, imagine never knowing — being left in limbo for years, Ghadi. None of that means I don't care about your brother, only that I loved mine too."

She watched how her words settled on him. Still nothing, or at least nothing he wanted her to know. She knew he studied transcendental mediation, so maybe that was how he pulled off that cold stoicism and hadn't sliced and diced her ass yet.

"Okay, I'm leaving," she nodded to him and turned.

"Delightful," his words stopped her. She pushed her hope down as she turned to face him.

"Stay away from my brother."

"I'll let him decide that." She returned and walked away.

"Trust me. It wouldn't be any different from Cali. I think he made himself clear by leaving you there." She kept walking, shame and humiliation cloaking every step.

* * *

A WEEK LATER...

"He'll do it." Delightful's cousin Angelique promised, plopping down on the bed. "I promised to make him some sweet potato pie. That boy is a food slut and will do things for food. Plus, he loves you and is tired of you moping around here killing our energy." She made broad circles in the air with her fingers for emphasis.

"Umm, okay thanks. Super harsh, too." She jumped from the bed, unwrapping her headscarf, making sure the two braids her youngest cousin, Skye, had styled her hair in had not come undone. "Is he ready now?" She bent down, looking at her cousin through the mirror as she put on her lip gloss.

"Almost, he eating. He went to workout before he came home. Which is good. Chances of the family being there now are slim. The security detail is there. They won't say anything to 'The Legend' though. They idolize him. He can go anywhere in this city, even to FADE's hospital room."

Delightful nodded, knowing how well her cousin's reputation preceded him. He was a hard charging leader of CRU, the Criminal Retrieval Unit. He went after the worst of the worst. He'd apprehended some of the most dangerous criminals all over the country.

They headed down the steps through a parlor similar to the one of her childhood home next door. Everyone thought it odd that two sisters lived next door to each other, but it led to one of the most fun childhoods a kid could ever hope for, even though her cousins were eccentric to say the least. No one messed with them though because they were fierce, unapologetic and down right ruthless when it came to their family. Which included her and her sisters. Loyalty was everything to the Loves, their mothers' side of the family and if they thought she was wrong, they'd let her know but there wouldn't be any cross words outside the home.

"Your mom wants you to call her," Xander Rafe-Leroi growled as he drank his sweet tea before tucking into his dinner of smothered pork chops, green peas and mashed potatoes.

"How do you like my food, Rafe? You know I made that special for you."

"That's how I know you wanted something. When I called to see what was for dinner and Skye told me. I was like, 'What does she want?' Food is good though." He chuckled, sweeping mashed potatoes onto his fork and into his mouth.

"Whatever."

"Let's go." He stood to his full six-foot-five hieght patting a belly that was nothing but muscle. If she ate like he just did, she wouldn't be unable to move for being so full. He earned the right though after pulling a full shift with his team then going to work out.

"I really appreciate you," she cringed. "I know you've had a long day."

He was already waving her words away heading to the door. "Nah, anyone looking at you knows how you are about FADE and I get why Ghadi feels the way he does. I also know

FADE and if he cares about you like I bet he does, he'd want to see you. No matter how y'all ended things, that was before he almost died. That will change even the coldest man."

The ride over was a blur of city lights and a mix of conversation about some of the crazy cases he had that could be a prime time show to rival anything she saw on tv.

"When we get there don't say anything. I know these guys. They may or may not recognize you, but there is a code. If I don't acknowledge your existence it'll be like you are invisible. I'll hang out and talk to them and you go in and see your guy." She had to double-time to keep up with him as he gave her instructions.

They walked down corridor after corridor. She noticed that they were no longer in the ICU but another swanky area of the hospital. She'd heard that rich people had entire suites in hospitals for everything from specialized treatments and secret plastic surgeries. Urban legend, she guessed it wasn't. She was sure some millionaire donated a vast sum for this wing. This was a recovery wing, yet it had a really posh atmosphere. Nothing had been skimped on. Not that she could turn up her nose at the hospital in any regard it was a class one trauma center and a teaching hospital.

They finally came upon a small troop of police around what looked like a command center. She pushed herself to walk alongside Rafe with a nonchalant air.

"Hey, Sarge." One of the younger officers came over ,when his eyes skated to her there was a spark of recognition. Whether from her winning an Oscar or having Ghadi putting a BOLO on her she didn't know.

"Hey partner, are you guys staying safe?" Rafe turned fully to the officer with his back now to her heading to the command desk where the other officers were huddled. It was obvious they were in the middle of a shift change.

She saw another officer standing sentry at what must be

FADE's door. She paused looking at him and he gave her no response but held his body as if he were more than ready for her to try.

"Moses." The officer's head perked up, then quirking an eye at her headed over to the command desk.

Looking neither left nor right, she headed straight for the room. Pushing the door open, grateful for barley a whisper of sound, she slipped inside.

The room was dim. There were no monitors. Nothing was attached to him, not even a blood pressure monitor.

"They are letting me go home tomorrow."

Her spirit almost left her body hearing his voice raspy from probably the intubation reach her ears. She slapped her hand over her mouth to suppress the scream that almost escaped. That would negate the whole sneaking in to see him effort if she were to have police rushing in here because she was screaming like she was being attacked.

She dropped her hand and walked over to the end of the bed, seeing him clearly for the first time since he'd left her at the cottage.

It was obvious he'd been through a terrible ordeal. He'd lost at least twenty pounds if not more. His skin was ashened. His muscles stood out in stark relief against his tawny skin. There were bruises all over his chest, which he hadn't bothered to cover. His eyes were half-cast, but his gaze was steady and cold. All the passion that was there before was gone.

A surge of desperation pounded in her heart. Her mind was seized by regret so much regret and shame.

"FADE..."

"Why are you here Delightful, now?" His eyes cast around for what she didn't know until they rested on the water decanter at the end of the bed. She hurried over to the plastic container and poured water for him, noting that her hands trembled a little. She handed it to him, nodding in return to his murmured, "Thanks."

"I was here the next day. I came with Sadiq and Hasan. I talked to your mom, and she gave me an update." She saw surprise register on his face before she continued. "I know how we ended things and I know I had no right to come but I couldn't, no I wouldn't allow you to go through this alone and without knowing how sorry I am and how much I care about you. I had to make sure you were all right."

His hand fisted the sheet, leaving a tight crumbled ball before he smoothed it out.

"I am well on my way to recovery. You can go back to California now," his voice was like death. No emotion. Never had he been this shut down.

"Come on FADE," she whisper-shouted leaning toward him. "You know why I'm here." Her breath caught when he lashed out like a striking cobra and pulled her to him.

"To make sure you get your movie made," he sneered, his eyes iced over shards of amber, cutting her heart to shreds. She must have been deluding herself that he looked weak. His grip with a little more pressure would be crushing.

"You're going to rip your stitches," she warned, her hand holding pressed against his chest.

"Getting shot is worse. You betraying me already ripped me apart," he murmured, his hand gentling at her nape.

"I don't want you to hurt yourself," she pleaded.

"No, you want to be the one to torture me. You came here to check on me looking like the best thing I ever tasted with your eyes wet with tears. Tell me Didi, where else can I get you wet?" He bit his bottom lip as his eyes trailed down to hers.

She closed hers eyes against the filthy thoughts bombarding her. She shook her head. "Dude, you are recovering. You almost died..."

"And my last thought was of you," he ground out. "Not my mom, dad, Flower, Willow or Ghadi. Not how much money I'd made or what I've accomplished. You. It was you." His lips claimed her. Devoured her. She had no recourse but to accept his plunder. He'd take her soul if he could. His mouth slanted. Paradise was his promise, and her body responded. No thought given to his condition, his leg or his head. She wanted to get in his skin. He hissed as her grip tightened, his own hand gripping her ass. His fingers dipping into her crevice from behind, rubbing where she ached. She moaned. He pulled away looking at her seeing way more than she wanted. She cast her gaze down to keep something for herself. She felt her emotions spiraling. She would either breakdown or climb on top of him at any moment.

"Don't look away. Let me see you, Didi," he commanded. It was one she couldn't obey.

"You're still fucking running," his disdain dripped from every word.

"I'm not. We're done. You said that. I won't let you just use me, FADE." She kept her voice firm, belying everything that had just transpired between them. "I won't let you break me."

He eased up to a sitting position and quirked his eyes. "I can't fuck you like I want to here, anyway.It's too many guys out there."

"I didn't come here for that. I came to check on you and apologize," she said.

"I don't accept it." He reached for his water again and took a sip. His eyes never left hers and she felt the truth of his words. She blinked. He blinked back taunting her.

"I understand. You're perfectly right not to." She nodded. This she'd honestly didn't expect. She never thought he'd see her again. Now he was making it clear he meant what he said in the cottage. She backed away from the bed. He grabbed her wrist. She knew he could feel the threadiness of her pulse. He caressed her there like he relished her upset. She was frozen as his icy gaze ate her up. This was the ruthless motherfucker they whispered about. This is who came at night and handled things. Ended things with a glacial aplomb that would leave you broken. He hid this side of himself when he cherished her. No more. She was getting the devil she invoked with her scheme to expose him as Justice's killer. Now he wouldn't be satisfied until she lay upon his altar.

"I have an entire floor leased in the John Hand Building you can give me your apology there." Cool words and colder eyes met her when she could finally pull her eyes away from his thumb drawing lazy circles on her pulse.

"Your family won't want me there. They probably have my picture up all over the place." She huffed.

"Let me worry about my family." He let her go and settled back into the bed. "I'll text when I'm ready for your apology."

She was contrite, yes, but if he thought he could just dismiss her he would be disappointed.

"So, let me get this right. My apology here is not good enough, but if I come over to there it is? Nah, fella, I ain't doing it. I'm not some side-chick to be running after you. Nope." She was brimming with outrage that he'd even dare suggest it.

"Sadiq will be eager to know my decision to end this film. He thinks it will flop anyway because of all this BS you've stirred up. I'll tell him to break it to Lovie-Belle, or would you rather?"

He let that little bomb drop like it was nothing.

"I did't come here to keep the movie on track." Hurt raged inside of her at his words. Still, he believed she was only there for the movie.

"It matters to you if it's cancelled. The studio wants to pull it. The timing is bad. Hasan thinks we can salvage it.

He's a minority in that thinking. However, they feel I have a brilliant comeback story with this happening. It's my call." He spread his hands, nonchalant as hell.

"You'd hurt Lovie-Belle," she challenged, but it came out as a plea.

"Wrong. You would." The clap-back was as hard as the chest she's just gripped.

"Fine." She gritted her nose stung, her eyes burned.

His next words crushed her. "The movie, your sister, even your family. Never FADE."

She shook her head, backing away from him moving toward the door.

He'd twisted every thing.

"Have your phone on." His words reached her as the door closed.

*J*ust Get It Done

"ONE MORE, come on FADE, you got this." Marchellis urged him. Sweat was popping out in places all over his body that he'd didn't even know were possible. His knee was on fire, his back ached, his head fucking hurt. He marshaled every once of strength he had to finish the last quarter squat, not just pushing past the pain, the hurt, pain and disappointment he felt but harnessing it for the power he needed to get his body back. To get his life back. Desolation lurked in the corners of his mind like a wrath, but he could not, would not give in to it. Despair would never fucking own him again. He'd promised himself this when he lost Justice and her the first time. He would not give into it again. He owed it to his friend to live, hell he owed it to himself for every sacrifice he'd ever made. He couldn't stop. He wouldn't stop. He was going to get his life back. Bet.

He'd been eviscerated in the press for the past month and a half since his release from the hospital. He was too busy to focus on anything but his recovery to allow those distractions to bother him, but now it was affecting his bottom line. The IPO launch was stalled. Every backer they had fled in the wake of the scandal and the fallout from the shooting. And with Flower out of commission with her stellar negotiating skills, they were at a real disadvantage. They were lucky they'd diversified early enough in tech or they'd have to shut down.

He was his brand, and his brand was trash now. In an industry that prided itself on street cred his was blown to smithereens. A snitch. It couldn't be borne. Nobody would work for him or collaborate with him. All the artists under his label were in revolt, wanting out of their contracts and he didn't blame them. The impact on Ghadi's career was the same and his brother had more to lose because he was still releasing and touring along with his other duties at Creative Chaos. He had a mega tour coming up early next dear with some to the top groups in the world and some were now hinting they didn't want to be associated with him. Ghadi's rep stood on its own. He'd never distance himself from FADE and it was having a negative effect on him. True to form and loyal to his core, he didn't even bring it up to him, he just shouldered it as always.

Only the most loyal of their fellow artists remained true, and only behind scenes. No one but Lyric was sticking their neck out. She had the clout of being the biggest female artist out for the last decade. Her word, her network of supporter's who self named themselves 'Lyric's Notes' were the only thing keeping his ass from being canceled. She was only one of the few people who knew what really happened, and only after he'd had no choice to tell her after he was shot. He could have gone to his grave with people never knowing what he'd done to make Justice's murderer play for what he'd done. Armed with that knowledge, Lyric did everything within her vast influence to help him as he recovered.

"You good?"

He refocused on the task at hand and rose back to his start position and dead eyed his friend. "I know you mean well and I appreciate you taking the time to help with my training while it's off season but I kinda hate your ass right now."

"Good. That means it's working." Marchellis grinned big, the light capturing the blinged out cap he used to cover the chipped tooth he'd gotten from his college basketball days. "Look at you. You put on twenty pounds of muscle. You'll be giving me some competition with the ladies."

"Oh, really? Nobody wants a big giant goofball following them around." FADE looked over to see his sisters come in. Willow was laughing at her own joke and Flower had even mustered a smile. He was glad to see her. He made this space available for both of them to work out as they recovered from their injuries. His heart squeezed at the ordeal his sister, who had always been such a bright light, had gone through. He wished she'd talk about it, but knew she would in her own time.

"Aww, hush little girl." His thousand kilowatt smile warmed more as he walked over and greeted the women with a bear hug that had them squirming trying to get away from his sweat laden body.

"Ew," they both cried in unison. Their faces crunched in disgust, which made him laugh as Marchellis hugged them closer.

"And you're kind of tangy too with your stinky self." Willow pushed him and he lunged for her which she easily dodged and had him stalking her around the room. They were funny together. Good together like he and Delightful could have been had things been different.

"I know that look." Flower looked at him with sadness lingering in her eyes as she approached and pulled a towel from a nearby rack so she could begin her own workout.

"What look?" He wiped his head and neck with a towel.

"That look that says you're pining after that ol' no good girl." She shook her head at him like he was pitiful.

"Yeah? Well then, I've seen it on your face too. Care to tell us who he is?" He kept his tone gentle, but there was no fooling her. She knew him too well. He'd kill the mother-fucker who put that look of desolation on his baby sister. She wasn't broken, but she was definitely bruised.

"That will be a triple-double nopity, nope, nope. You are dangerous and Ghadi is diabolically slick. So, no. I'll pass big brother." She went over to the high-end stationary bike he'd gotten for his knee replacement and began to enter her workout.

"I'm going back to New York," she told him as she began to peddle. "I don't know why you're still here." She stopped and smacked her head. "Ohh yes, I do." She rolled her eyes and started to peddle in earnest.

He laughed at her shaking his head. She was well on the mend if she could make fun of him.

"Why? You can telework if that's what you want." He asked, though not surprised by her choice.

"It's time for me to start my own thing. I was with Bridget and Evangelina in Japan and they are doing so much. They have their own company, Bite. They love it." The way her eyes lit up, he knew he couldn't do anything but support her.

"Just give me until the IPO launches and then I will help you do whatever you want to do," he promised.

"Deal." She blew him a kiss and got serious with her workout. She was getting stronger every day, and he was proud of her. She motivated him in so many ways, always giving one hundred percent with any task. He just wanted to see her smile like she used to.

He turned to see Marchellis watch with rapt attention as Willow showed off one of her ballet moves. There was a lot unsaid going on there, but he wouldn't interfere. He knew his friend wouldn't hurt his sister, just as he would've never hurt Delightful.

Marchellis looked over and caught him looking at them play and turned away from Willow looking chagrined. "All right." He clapped his hands, walking back over to where he stood. "Let's get some treadmill work done."

FADE groaned but got on the machine under his friend's watchful gaze.

* * *

"Damn," he groaned, grabbing his leg as the muscles spasmed. He pulled the covers off his legs. He watched the muscles bunch and jump on their own accord under his hands. It was too late to call a masseuse. He pressed the tightest knot with his thumb for ten seconds to try to release the cramp. The doctors had told him the more he pushed himself that this would happen as his body tried to heal itself. It hurt like hell, but he didn't want to take the muscle relaxers they had prescribed him or the pain killers. He always did his best to keep his body clean. He'd never done drugs, knowing the havoc they'd reeked on his community and on the lives of some of his fellow artists. He never smoked and rarely drank. He defied the perception of what the wild life of a rap star was.

His phone chimed. The same person who'd been texting him from the moment he was released from the hospital. He'd been too physically weak to see her. He'd needed time and space away from her and what had happened to him to see things clearly. He wasn't weak anymore, his body was nearly healed. His mind? He was torn between wanting retribution and wanting to hold her.

Didi: Are you ready for your apology?

HE LOOKED DOWN at those words for an eternity, just as he had every night. Every night it was a struggle. He battled with himself the moment he got out of his sickbed until now. The memory of her tortured him — her taste, her touch, her pussy. He missed the smell of her hair, the mix of tropical and the earthiness of coco butter that always seemed to follow her with each sway and shake of hair. Her smile, when she deigned to gift him with one, he found in his dreams. Every night. His insomnia which he'd struggled with all his life because his mind could never stop making music was back full force. Then when he did dream it was of her. Their pleasure and her betrayal. Last night it was her tears. He found himself waking to his own. The cottage in California had done nothing but make him want her more.

FADE: Are you ready to give it?

HE CLOSED HIS EYES. He wished she said, go to tell. He knew she wouldn't. That movie meant everything to her. It would solidify her career and that of Lovie-Belle. There was nothing she'd not do for her sisters. He loved that about her. He loved a lot of things about her he readily admitted. Would she ever do anything for him?

· · ·

DIDI: Yes

FADE: I'm waiting.

Didi: Ok

HE WAS ABOUT to see what his forgiveness meant to her. He tossed the phone down on the bedside table.

"WHAT ARE YOU DOING HERE?"

Delightful turned to the sound of Flower's voice to her left as she entered the building. She looked over to the white marble columns and saw her friend if she could still be called that standing like a tiny sentinel with her arms crossed in front of her.

"Hey, Flower. I heard you were ill the same time FADE got hurt." Delightful walked over to her.

"You mean when you almost got him murdered? He wasn't hurt Delightful, he nearly died." She took a handkerchief out of her pocket and wiped her nose before turning burning eyes back on her. Her movements were shaky, and it was obvious she had being crying hard.

"Are you okay?" Delightful moved toward her, worry racking her. She should call FADE. Flower was unraveling before her eyes. "Hey, hey, Flower..." She stopped when a hard hand was thrown up before she could get any closer.

"I'll be all right." She fumbled with the handkerchief again and had somehow managed to get it tangled with her phone. As she tried to unravel it her phone tumbled and clattered landing face up right in front of Delightful's feet.

Looking down into the face of a gorgeous Asian couple, she picked up the phone and handed back to her teary friend.

"Beautiful couple. Are they friends of yours?" She watched as Flower's face crumbled before her eyes.

"No. No, they are not my friends." She watched her press the sleep button and place it in the pocket of her jeans. Before going back to her original query. "Why are you here?"

"Your brother said he's ready to hear my apology."

Flower was already shaking her head. "You mean to tell me, you held a grudge for twelve years over some mess he didn't have anything to do with yet he's here forgiving your treacherous tail? Jeeze Louise!"

Delightful cringed hearing the cold, hard truth. "He said nothing about forgiving me, only that he'd be willing to allow me to apologize." The need to defend him spike up in her like a geyser. Not even his family could besmirch him before her eyes. She'd never allow it.

She'd been doing her best to counter the mess she'd caused working with Lyric, the Al Rasheeds and her industry contacts to clear FADE's name. She'd had to keep it as under-cover as possible because Ghadi had initiated a scorched earth policy against her. He'd somehow found out that she'd been to FADE's hospital room and had let her know in no uncertain terms that she was to stay away from his family or he'd make his presence felt with her family. She knew he meant it. She didn't blame him. Only she couldn't let things with FADE end like this. She wanted to see him and try her best to make things right.

"Why did you do it? I was rooting for you," Flower demanded. "Why would you set out to hurt him after he's done so much for you and your family?"

"I told my parents, and I was wrong for that period. Would I do it again? Yes. My parents had a right to know. Nothing I will ever do will make up for how I let FADE and you guys down. All I can do is try to make it right and say I'm sorry. FADE agreed to do the movie and we are grateful. It's totally up to him what happens next." She watched every emotion flit across Flower's face from anger and confusion to finally settle on sadness.

"What is it?" She leaned in, keeping her tone soft as not to agitate the already upset woman.

"That's something you need to discuss with FADE." She waved her away.

"Is it some type of secret? What else has FADE done for my family? Is that some kind of secret too?" A slow realization crept into her mind as she watched Flower struggle with herself without bursting forth with what she knew.

"My dad's job?" Delightful just pulled that from the air. But it had been right after her brother died. Then her dad finally got the promotion with the power company that he'd been qualified for and denied for years.

Flower nodded. "The chief called in a favor because FADE asked them to in exchange for his cooperation."

The news settled on Delightful like a leaden weight, knowing what that meant.

"Miracle's scholarship to the Autism Academy and everything that followed? Berkeley? Why? He'd made sure that Justice got credit for his songs on the first three albums and everyone he sampled a little from afterwards."

"Why?" Flower scoffed. "He made a promise to Justice. He's loyal. Though now you have everyone thinking he isn't. He was going to make sure you guys were just taken care of no matter what. Aside from trying to make it, his sole purpose in life was taking care of you guys. You didn't see him after Justice died. You wouldn't see him and he got it. He ensured that you soared. There's nothing in your life he's not smoothed the way for. All that time you shunned him, never took his calls and acted like he didn't exist. He was having your back like Justice's would have had mine." She stepped away again, her eyes sheened with tears as she shook her head. Still not done. "I'm going back to New York tomorrow because staying here is not good for me right now. I need to get back to work. If you hurt my brother again, you won't just have Ghadi to deal with."

"He asked me to come. I'm not here to hurt him." Her words held the conviction of her intentions, but she could tell they didn't sway Flower.

"Keep telling yourself that if it makes you feel better. Part of you still blames him. There is no way you held that for twelve years and it evaporated overnight."

"The moment I saw him, something shifted. I always knew deep down I wouldn't be able to hold on to my anger once I saw him. Maybe that's why I stayed away from him." She shrugged and moved towards the elevator.

"Don't tell him I was down here and you saw me crying. He'd only worry unnecessarily," Flower called over to her as she pressed the call button for the elevator.

"Don't tell Ghadi, I was here and you have a deal." She bit her inner cheek to keep from smiling at her former friend's fury.

"Whatever." Flower rolled her eyes in disgust.

Delight stepped in the elevator and shrugged as the doors closed.

Just Sorry

THE ELEVATOR OPENED onto a dim-lit floor. You'd think you were in a New York City high-rise with less obstruction. The wall of windows of the penthouse loft showed all of downtown Birmingham on one side, then all the way to Red Mountain and surrounding areas on the other side. The city was all sparkling lights from up here. She could see every major landmark, she thought as she walked deeper into the building. At a distance the museum shone in white marble and the park with the missing the Confederate obelisk the people demanded be torn down could barely be made out. This was home and always would be, she realized as she'd waited for his call these many weeks. Having spent that time with her cousins, she'd seen what she missed after leaving and never really coming back after college. Her family and culture were here. This was her soft place to fall. The place to forgive and be forgiven.

"I'm back here." FADE called. She scrunched her face up at the way his voice rasped, then picked up her pace as she followed the sound. He sounded like he was in pain.

"Are you okay?" She came into the bedroom area and saw him in a massive bed sitting up clutching his thigh.

"Muscle spasms," he grunted. "The doc said they are a sign of healing but they are killing me."

She didn't know what sound she made, but he looked at her for the first time. "Why are you in pajamas?"

"This is the writer's uniform, don't ya know? I was working late and totally not thinking you were in forgiveness mode tonight." She kept her tone light as she moved closer.

"You know my dad used to have muscle spasms all the time when he was a line-man for the power company and mom would run him a mineral bath. Do you have some rock salt?" She stood beside him and brushed his hands away and started manipulating the corded muscle.

"Yeah, mom bought a ton different types before she left. My wound had not healed by then, so I never used them. Flower got all kinds of stuff as well. I have a compression boot but I can't sleep with that damn thing on." He sounded so miserable to her. Compassion and guilt had her swallowing against the tears that threatened to break free. How could he ever forgive her for the part she played in the pain he was enduring?

Flower's words snuck in at that moment, compounding the feelings. After everything he'd done for her and her family, this was her thanks, almost crippling him and causing him countless nights of pain.

"Would you like me to make you a mineral bath?" she

asked, not knowing if she wanted him to say yes or no. She just wanted him to stop hurting, not cause him more pain.

"Yeah," he whispered.

She moved away from him and looked around, not seeing an entrance to the bathroom.

"It's through there." He nodded to the wall to the right of the bed. Puzzled, she walked around the bed to the wall and looked over to him. As she approached, the door slid open.

"It is accessibility friendly. I am getting all Creative Chaos outfitted like this. You don't think about it when it doesn't affect you. I was grateful when I didn't have to fumble with a doorknob while using my crutches." She nodded at him because neither had it ever occurred to her. "You're right. That would be fantastic if you did that."

"No if. I'm doing it. I told Ghadi and Flower to make it happen before I got back. I also wrote a memo across Creative Chaos about the plans in the future with our disabled colleagues in mind. I told Sadiq and Hasan they also needed to make accessibility changes on the set." She watched as he lay back, resting on the now smushed pillows behind him as she went into the bathroom. It was wall to wall white marble with thin pink veins swirling throughout. There was a wall shower with all marble and a rimless clawfoot tub that was big enough for three grown men to sit in.

After retrieving the various mineral bath products, Grace'd left she ran the water and poured the one that smelled best to her in the water and swished it around until it dissolved. She put towels on the warmer, then walked back into the bedroom.

"Why didn't you take the muscle relaxers?" She asked, looking at the nearly full bottle beside the bed.

"I like to keep my body free of intoxicants and I don't like how they make me feel. I also have to make three more songs for the movie." She looked over at him and he responded with a quirk of an eyebrow.

"Do you need your crutches?" She watched as he eased himself to the edge of the bed completely naked mind you, his dick just hanging long and semi-hard beckoning for a kiss or cuddle. She tore her eyes away. She did not need that kind of aggravation or temptation in her life right now.

"Nah, I can just hang on you for a little bit." He beckoned her closer.

"FADE, dude, you're like huge. I won't be able to keep us from falling." She moved back and grabbed his crutches from the wall beside the bed, holding them out to him.

He dropped his hand, his eyes tinged with disappointment, and took them from her. He heaved himself up on the crutches as she backed up, giving him room. She stayed by his side as he made his way to the bathroom. He was right about the convenience and necessity of the automatic door. She couldn't imagine how he'd made it those first days and maintained his dignity when he needed privacy.

"You're right about the doors. I'm proud of you for doing that for your people at Creative Chaos." Her words dried up as his eyes slid over to her as he moved to the door. She didn't know what that look meant.

"I hate these things. I overdid it today working with Marchellis and I'm playing for it now." He sighed, stepping over the tub's rim as she held the crutch he used for support. He hissed as he stepped in. "Damn girl, you've got this water hot as hell. You're trying to kill all my babies," his chuckle mixed with a groan as he slid down into the water. The fragrance wafted up with the smell of citrus and bergamot. Steam rose from the water, which was just cloudy enough so she could only see the barest hint of his body below the waist.

"I guess you prefer them swallowed," she quipped.

His stone-face countenance broke into a thousand bits as he threw his head back and laughed until he had to wipe tears away.

His head fell back as she pulled the sleeves up her arms. She reached into the warm water, taking the knotted muscled and massaged him. She saw the pain painted across his face and her heart broke bit by bit. She let her touch tell the story of her sorrow. In that moment she didn't care if he ever forgave her only that she could give him some type of comfort.

"I'm sorry for mistreating you." She knew it needed to be said. She'd wrong him and they both knew it.

He just watched her. The silence was like a tomb. She turned away, concentrating on loosening the muscle. They seemed determined to remain bunched, as stubborn as she and the man she was helping. She pressed deep into the muscle like she'd seen her mother do countless times when her dad had come from an interminable night of replacing power lines after tornadoes. Press for ten second then relax and massage until the tissue was once again pliable.

She let her gaze travel up his body. He'd gained some of his weight back, but he was not back at his full weight and probably not his strength yet. Try to tell her body that, though. Because it wanted to be strung-out on him. The only reason they'd not gone any further that night in the hospital was because he'd stop them. He could have played her like he did the piano or the soundboard in the studio. She was powerless to deny him and not knowing what lay ahead, she couldn't put herself out there. He'd say she was running, but she was trying to save what little she had left.

"Does that feel better?" She saw he'd totally relaxed against the tub.

"So much better," he murmured, his amber gaze settling on her. Her breath shunted. Heat bloomed in her heart. The coldness was gone. He looked wary. As if she would cause him further harm. She the writer didn't have the words now. What words could she say at this point? She wasn't worthy to utter them. She almost caused him to die. That he'd even see her was a testament to his love for Justice. His loyalty knew no bounds.

"I can see it in your eyes, Didi."

Her heart skipped.

"What?" Her eyes darted away then back. She tried to hold them there but failed and pushed back to stand and get him a towel.

He stood and stepped out, bearing most of his weight on his uninjured leg and propped-up by the crutch.

She busied herself drying him, hoping he'd go back to silent mode. She tossed that towel aside and wrapped another around his waist. She got mango butter and rubbed it over his chest, then back, leg, and buttocks. She held it out to him. "You can finish." She rubbed over his arms and shoulders. As she came up to his neck she froze catching the heated glare of his beautiful gaze.

"You're still running."

"You said I could come and apologize." She handed him the other crutch and followed him back to the bedroom. She rushed past him and went over to the side he'd been on and switch out the pillows with those on the opposite side and fluffed them.

"Consider all of this your apology. I appreciate it." He tossed the towel and got in the bed. She could see his exhaustion pouring from every part of him.

"Um, okay." She rolled her sleeves down and tucked the cover around him. Casting around for words... anything. "I'm still sorry for putting you in danger," her voice broke. She broke. She bit her lip til she tasted blood.

He sat back up and grabbed her arm.

"Stay."

She nodded and hurried around to the other side of the bed and climbed in.

"Lights." He called out into the room and they instantly dimmed blanketing the room in darkness save for the city lights.

"Are you going to call shades or something? Because that bright light is going to trigger my migraine in the morning."

"They automatically darken when the sun comes up. Come here," he grumbled.

She scooted over and tucked herself beneath his chin. Suddenly tiredness swamped her. She'd been writing all day on another project now that she was done with the Just Forever screenplay and only had a consulting role on the film now. They'd contact her if a scene wasn't working, but that was unlikely. She'd been told the script had been green-lit, but she'd been left wondering what was happening. Lovie-Belle had told her it was business as usual but she'd hadn't had the final say and Delightful refused to get her hopes up until FADE spoke about it tonight.

"What changed your mind?" She lifted her head to look at him. He'd been staring at the ceiling.

"Who says I changed it?" He cut his eyes toward her then sighed so deep she felt it. "Sadiq demanded we move ahead because of all the work Lovie-Belle has put into it. It seems she's made quite an impression on the Al Rasheed brothers and their team."

"So this is still about your promise to Justice," she mused, cupping her chin in her hand.

"Is that what you think?" His look turned intent again. "That I did for Justice?"

"I don't know you tell me."

"I stopped answering to people a long time ago. I run a corporation, little girl. I am a business. The business calls for me to put aside my feelings to save my brand. The movie is the sound way to go," he spoke with hard conviction. He was doing for his brand. He was reclaiming his name.

"Well, that makes sense." She was glad he'd released himself from his obligation to Justice. She wouldn't want him to make a decision that could be ruinous just based on what he felt would help her.

The silence stretched. She felt the heaviness of sleep pressing down on her. Her eyes were drifting when she thought she her him whisper, "I did it for you."

*J*ust a Little Bit More

HE FELT the softness of her body pressed against his and buried his nose in her curls. She'd not come to stay and had not thought to cover her hair. She was going to regret that and probably be mad as all get out, but he was in heaven breathing in the intoxicating smell of her curls. She was delectable. He couldn't stop the groan that rumbled through him. His body knew what he needed. Her. Delightful Howard was right here in his bed where she'd belonged after twelve years of running from him like she was a gazelle and he a lion on the plains of the Serengeti. She was here, all softness and curves. That thought made his heart do all kinds of crazy things. There wasn't a man alive who would not taste her. And he like the lion wanted to feast on her. Everything fell away.

"Didi," He whispered pulling her closer. Her body was

flush with his. He kissed her curls, snuggling deeper in to the crush of softness.

"Hm?" Her voice was rough silk in the morning. She pushed back against him. "You're so warm," she sighed, digging deeper into the pillow.

"I need you." His arms tightened around her but other than that he held back. He wouldn't push her. She shifted around until she was facing him. He looked down into her sleep drenched eyes. "So fucking beautiful." He watched the sleepy smile spread across her race. A familiar emotion bloomed in his heart. It had always been there. He'd never spoken it aloud and probably wouldn't today, but his heart acknowledge it as it had all those years ago. There would never be another.

"You're not so bad yourself." She winked up at him and leaned in and kissed his neck. She sucked in the skin at the base and he felt himself lengthen.

She eased him back and climb atop straddling him placing light kisses around his neck until she moved up and slipped his earlobe in her mouth lightly sucking it adding a naughty nibble. That's when his dick jumped. She giggled moving to his lips. He opened for her completely at ease with her taking charge. Everything about her was soft, plush and hot. He could feel her heated center pressing against his belly. He ached for her to move lower yet let her take the lead. Her plump lips pressed in, teasing his tongue then taking him deep, mimicking the head she gave so well. He wanted to push her down on his dick so badly instead he breathed deep trying to calm himself.

She immediately rewarded him, repositioning until she settled on him fully with only the thin layer of her pajamas separating them. He could rip them and have her taking his dick in a second, he mused as the kiss deepened, their tongues mingling, sliding, him taking her and she taking him in return. A sensual heat rose between them. She moved her heated core against him. He could feel the stiffened peaks of her nipples rubbing against his chest, teasing him. Taunting.

"I'm at a disadvantage," he whispered. Lifting to suck a protruding bud into his mouth. She flexed her hips, pushing herself along the ridge of his dick with an excruciating grind.

"Damn, Didi," he growled pulling back and switched to the other side to suck the other nipple into his mouth. Again she flexed, and he welcomed her delicious punishment and even became a willing participant arching his hips to meet her.

"How are you at a disadvantage?" She tilted her head like she didn't know exactly what she was doing to him.

"I'm naked and you have all your clothes on." The sway of her other breast distracted him. He smooth the material up her sides and over her head. She lifted her arms to help him. He tossed the top away and went back to the view of smooth brown skin before him. Her breast beckoned him. He pushed the mounds together.

"Lean down."

He captured both tips in his mouth. He felt her drenching him as he took her in long pulls. She created a rhythm all her own. The snap and swirl of her hips were going to be his undoing.

"Take those pants off," he commanded, urging them down her hips.

She hurried to comply, moving off him. His eyes rounded when she stood over him. His dick rose and slapped against his belly, bouncing up in anticipation.

"Where are your condoms?" He leaned over and reached into the drawer, his eyes never leaving the image she presented as she stood atop his bed with her legs spread just enough to show how much she wanted him.

He tore open the wrapper with his teeth then grabbed the

root pumping up then smoothed the condom down from tip to base. She stepped over him. He'd experienced a lot of positions, but the sight of her slowly descending into a split would always top the list. His breath seized in his chest, "My God." She was hot. Her pussy looked succulent and was open to receive him. He wanted her skin to skin. He closed his eyes against her slowly taking him. He gripped her waist and surged, meeting her. Her grip, the way her muscled flexed around his dick made his toes curl. He was so close to coming he had to grit his teeth. "Your pussy is going to kill me. Damn. Are you all right? You're so fucking tight, Didi." Was he rambling? He couldn't think straight. His muscles tightened, and he had to rein himself in. She was the stuff dreams were made of and she was his.

"I'm good. You did a superb job getting me ready for this gigantic dick." Then she leaned forward, gripping his chest for balance, and kept descending until their bodies were flush chest to breast. The fit was perfect. From the moment they danced, he knew they'd be together like this. She rubbed her body along his, her hips rising and falling causing a sensual heat and an ached that his body had no choice but to chase. He met her thrust for thrust. Bodies slick.

"I want to see you taking my dick."

She rose, bringing her feet up to either side and braced her hands on his thighs.

"Ride me, Didi. Fuck me." He knew he sounded like he was pleading, but he couldn't bring himself to care. He needed her, had wanted her through his anger and his pain of recovery.

She took command. She was a goddess riding him like Queen Nzinga going into battle, her undulations slow then picking up speed driving him crazy, taking him to the brink. Over and over she took him. The tight squeeze of her pussy like a punishing kiss, killing and giving life simultaneously.

His toes curled. He reached between her legs and circled her protruding clit with his thumb, rubbing her wetness in around. Then with quick upward brushes he watched as she broke apart. Her nails digging into his thighs. She fell forward. "Your turn." She gasped. He need no further encouragement as he held her tight and fucked deep inside her welcoming warmth. She moaned again as he grazed her G-spot. He raised knees thrusting.

"FADE," she cried.

"I've got you," he soothed her but gave her no quarter. He buried his head in the crush of curls. Holding her tight, he saw pleasure cascaded over her body. His seed erupted from his body in hot bursts.

He held her for a long time. He could feel the chill on her skin and pulled the covers over them. He could feel her heartbeat slowing down, taking on a less erratic beat. Her breathing deepened. He looked down, watching as she slept. Part of him couldn't believe he was here holding her. A strange elation crept into his heart. He called himself ten times a fool. A chump. He was holding her, had made love to her. Gave her his body and took hers and if she offered him more he'd lap it up.

He'd guided his life on what Justice would do in so many instances. He knew Justice would have without a doubt have told his parents the truth just as Delightful had. He never would have allowed FADE's parents to languish in ignorance. His own mother had told him as much.

His sigh caused her to shift.

"Mmm," she moaned and her muscles clinched around his still sheathed dick. He eased her off him and discarded the condom.

He grabbed his crutches and headed to the bathroom. He looked at the mirror and cringed. He still wasn't quite up to his full weight. He resolved to work out harder and increase his calorie intake. He needed to get back to New York. The doctor had told him was almost ready to release him from his care and that could happen at his next appointment which was a week away. Then he'd be back in the game. The studio had set up interviews in print, online and especially on Black radio. There would be no type of comeback until he sat down with the judge and juries of hip hop. They were the most influential when it came to the careers of any rap star. They put you on and took you off. If you were whack you didn't get played. And no one's brand was whacker than his at the moment. Getting shot and surviving the murder attempt was the only thing that saved his career. He'd have to ride that sympathy all the way to the movie premier.

He stepped into the shower and turned it on, welcoming the spray that he'd hope would wash away the hurt, anger and yes, even fear that assailed him. "Please, God." He felt the tears burn his eyes. He let them come. He'd long ago gotten over the no crying bullshit. Smothering his feelings had almost killed him after they murdered Justice. He wouldn't allow that darkness to claim him again. He dropped his head against the marble. He could barely breathe under the water, but here he felt safe.

"FADE."

* * *

DELIGHTFUL WATCHED HIS HEAD TURN. He looked so lost. Broken. She stepped into the shower. She touched his arm. He turned into her open arms. His body bowed as he folded into her. She just held him close. She stroked his back, trying to pour comfort as an intention into him. He held her like he never wanted to let her go. And she didn't want him to. She wanted to hold him forever. She wanted to heal him like he'd healed her. She could admit that now. Just as she recognized how one sided everything was. He had only given. She took. What could she offer besides pleasure that he'd take after what she'd done? No one wanted to see themselves as a terrible person, but that was what she felt like. She might as well call herself, Lex.

He pulled away, not looking at her. "Uh-uh." She took his face in her hands. "We don't do that." She got on her tiptoes and kissed him. He drew her into him with a drugging plunder of her lips. He devoured her. His mouth slanted over hers.

Like a dry tinder thrown onto a barn fire they came together hot, burning, crackling, threatening to combust. His lips were everywhere and so were hers. There was not one inch of skin that their lips did not touch. She sobbed when his fingers slipped inside. Reaching down, she slicked her hand over his length from base to tip.

"FADE," she whimpered. So close. He took his hand away and turned her away towards the marble. Her breath caught as he thrust deep and slapped against her ass. Her face pressed against the wall as she worked against his length, offering herself up to him completely.

"Touch yourself," he ground out fucking so hard his hands would leave marks where he gripped her hips. "Come on your fingers and my dick." He commanded. Thier bodies were smacking hard as she did as he commanded, touching herself with deft flicks of hers fingers. Her breath was warm against the tile as she came crying out his name.

"Turn around."

She obeyed and saw that he was not done. She dropped to her knees and took him in her mouth. He held her head as he pushed deep into her throat over and over again spilling his essence.

They finished the rest of the shower with kisses, taking

turns to bathe one another. When they stepped out of the shower he gave her a heavy white robe that felt like a cloud.

She had him sit again to take pressure off his healing leg as she spread mango butter over his body.

"Do you have anything I can use on my hair? Your hair is a wavier curl pattern but I could be able to use it."

"I only need juices and berries." He winked, and she threw a towel at him.

"Yeah, Prince Akeem," she laughed. He knew she loved that movie.

He watched as she grumbled the whole time she detangled her hair, but he didn't mind she was so adorable when she fussed.

"C'mon." He threw his arm around her as they headed back to the bedroom, "I know you're hungry. Do you want Fish Market or Eagles?'

"What brave soul do you have willing to go all the way over to Eagles?" She dead eyed him.

"Everyone loves their food so... everyone." He quipped walking over to his side of the bed retrieving his phone.

"Don't worry about your clothes."

"Why?" She stopped as she bent to pick up her crumpled pajamas and looked over her shoulder at him as he typed into the phone. "You have on sweats."

"I'm going to be taking you right back out of them in a little bit. So why bother?" He quirked an eyebrow at her.

Her body liked the sound of that.

When he finished, he pocketed his phone and reached for her. He pulled her into his arms. He felt so good. He smelled clean, with the faintest hint of soap they'd used. She'd never tire of being held by him.

She had to drag herself away from that kiss. "You're a terrible influence."

She shook her head and pulled him along behind her into the living area.

They both stopped short when they saw Ghadi's long frame lounging in the all white seating area.

"What the hell is she doing here, FADE?"

CHAPTER 15

J ust Work It Out

DELIGHTFUL STOOD at FADE's side looking at Ghadi sprawled with his arms spread across the white linen sofa in the living area. He'd not let her hand go, in fact he moved closer to her.

"What are you doing here, Ghad? Who's minding the store?" He tucked her into his side and walked with her to the seating area. She made sure her robe was tucked in securely and faced her would-be judge.

"This is sight. By that, I mean this is some of the weakest shit I have ever seen. My brother hugged up with the chick who almost got him killed. Man, you don't care about your career at all, do you? Everyone is is talking about how they just know you're going to dead whoever did this. It's a miracle and by that I mean the Al Rasheeds and CC vast connections and bots zapping any mention of her involve-

ment that it hasn't gotten out yet. If they get a whiff of this…"
He shook his head, disgust blanketing his face.

"Are you done?" FADE asked. She could tell without looking over to him with her gaze trained on the coiled cobra before her, he'd spoken through clenched teeth. She didn't want to come between them but she knew that if she made a move to leave he'd see that as her running again. Her fingers curled into the softness of the robed as Ghadi threw his hands up in a 'what ever' motion. His eyes said so much more, though.

"I'm here to pickup our baby sister, remember her? The one who's loyal, loves you unconditionally, who's been here for your ass since day one. The woman who has foregone her dreams to help us with ours. The young lady who's heart is fucking broken while you were knee-deep up in this shorty. She's shown you who she is, bro." He might as well have slapped her. Heat rushed to her face as shame and humiliation slammed into her.

"Get out." FADE's words were cold. Her head swung to him, then back at Ghadi. The very thing she thought to avoid by remaining quiet was happening, anyway.

"No, FADE…"

"It's cool." Ghadi stood up facing his brother, wiry aggression wrapped within every fiber of his tall form. "Just know this. Flower was a mess this morning. She looked like she'd been up crying all night. You haven't been there for her," his voice was raw with worry and fury. She felt horrible hearing him say the very thoughts she'd had talking with their sister the previous evening.

FADE stepped closer to him, menace pouring off him. "We've never fought and we won't today because I'm going to excuse your disrespectful ass attitude toward Didi and me because it's obvious it stems from your concern for Flower. Never do this again, Ghadi. I'm handling my life. Flower has been here the whole time, just as you have held it down for us while we've been away. We have been taking care of each other." He crossed his arms over his chest.

"Funny you didn't have your Didi here to take care of you." He waved them away like he was over it. "I'm taking her home and having her see a therapist. This has gone on too long."

"Well, thank you thinking y'all are going to manage my life. I have been seeing one along with FADE." They'd been so engrossed in their argument they'd not noticed their sister had been standing just inside the suite. Delightful peeked around FADE's body blocking her, to see Flower standing before them in a white eyelet dress and pink heels. Gone was the distraught woman from last night replace by the calm COO of Creative Chaos. It was as if she'd allowed herself that one last ugly cry before she gathered herself and pulled together a semblance of the woman whom everyone knew to be the power behind her brothers. She speared Delightful with a look and walked around FADE with a package in her hands. "I figured you'd need these this morning," she said handing it to her.

"Thanks," she nodded, tucking the package under her arms.

"You saw each other last night?" FADE asked, his gaze swing back and forth between the two.

"Yeah," Flower said. "I asked her not to say anything because I was fine. It's okay that I cry guys even all night if I have to. Pushing my emotions down leads to bigger lows. So, I will cry when I feel like it, thank you very much." Her hands were on her hips, facing them like a little general.

"Wow," Ghadi gave a low laugh. "I guess you're ready to come back to work then?"

"I am. I've been away too long. And what happened to FADE falls squarely on my shoulders." She held up her hand when her brothers moved to deny it. "No, it is my responsibility, 'Yoroshiku onegaishimasu' as the Japanese term it. I learned that there and if I were anyone other than your sister, you would have fired me." The respect Delightful had for her former friend shot up hearing her words. Along with that thought slithered in the realization that she needed to do the same not just in her words but actions. She thought back to the picture of the gorgeous couple that Flower had on her phone and wondered how those people played into all of this.

"Well, we are not firing you. You can go back to New York, reorganize what you feel is lacking in security and require more training from the team." Ghadi nodded as FADE spoke.

Delightful watched as Flower took in those solemn words, then shook her head slightly and walked over into FADE's open arms. "I'm going to miss you, baby-girl." He bent low to hug her.

"Willow is the baby, not me." She pushed at him playfully before turning to Ghadi. "When are we leaving?"

"Whenever you are ready. The plane is fueled and waiting on us." That was his first smile in the whole time he had been there. "Next week I want some peach cobbler for coming all this way to get you."

"Okay, well this place doesn't have a valet so y'all need to go get my bags which are a lot because Bridget and Evangelina sent the rest of my things I left in my haste to get here," she ordered to her brothers. They rolled their eyes and grumbled but did what she said, heading to the door.

"And y'all make up or I'm telling daddy," she called to them as they reached the elevator.

Delightful saw they had obeyed her as they turned to face one another in low conversation as the doors closed.

"That has always worked." Flower turned to her. "I heard

what Ghadi said to you but I trust FADE enough to know that he will do what he's always done to protect his interest. I was all for having you fired and slapping a restraining order on you."

Delightful couldn't hide the stunned surprise that marked her features. "What changed your mind?"

"Nothing. FADE wouldn't do it. He still loves Justice and your family no matter what. He's given you a lot of leeway. You being here and being seen with him is not the best look. We have a plan and strategy that could possibly work to savage his legacy and our company, but it doesn't include you. So I'm asking you to leave him alone. To let him heal and get his life back. I hate to play the family card, but I will. He's done so much for y'all do it for him even if it hurts. He's not going to let you go. He loves you."

"You don't know how he feels." Delightful felt like the rug had been pulled out from under her.

"You're not an idiot or would it make you feel better if he were just using you and for what? Sex? He can get that anywhere. My brother has loved you forever, and I was so happy when you finally came back in his life, but you're problematic. I've been to therapy and I suggest you go as well. You're not dealing with Justice's death and what ever survivor's guilt you are experiencing is causing you to lay waste to everything that matters to you. You're stuck and now you're bringing my brother down and that I cannot allow."

Her words were like bombs of truth that blanketed every space that she'd inhabited, and Delightful could not duck and hide from those words. She'd made a mess of things and she'd not regretted anything she'd done before now because her cause had been pure, or so she thought.

"I needed to know what happened to Justice," she kept her

voice strong and unwavering despite the tumult she felt hearing Flower's words.

"You got that and more, but that wasn't enough. I wonder what will be. You resent FADE for living when your brother died. You wish it had been him lying in that road."

"Now, that's a lie. I would have never wished that on FADE. I loved him." She stepped closer to Flower. She was brimming with anger.

"And now?"

"I love him," she sighed clutching the package closer to her chest trying to ward off any more of Flower's truth bombs doing her more harm. She knew she would not stop til she drew blood.

"Well, you have a funny way of showing it."

"All right, I get it. You want me to leave him alone."

"No. I want you to do something for him for once. I told you about what he's done for you and your family all this time. Now you can do something for him. Let him heal free of feeling any obligation to anyone. Help him finally break this shackle of obligation that been hanging over him for twelve years."

"If I do that. He's going to think I'm not choosing him. That I'm disloyal. You just want us to not be together." Hearing the desperation in her own voice made her wince. Flower was making so much sense.

"Is this how you want him? Both of you broken?" Flower demanded, her eyes growing cold. "If you love him. You will do the work on yourself because you're too toxic. You're going to always find a way to mess it up. Trust me. I have been there and to be honest I'm still trying to find my way out at times." Her honesty almost broke Delightful, as she saw the anguish and shame flit across her face.

"Flower, I know you are hurting and if you ever want to

talk, I'm here..." her words were cut off as she was nearly hug-tackled.

"I know and I know you are still hurting. You are vibrating with it. One day we are going to be best friends again, I know it." Flower squeezed her and stepped away.

She could find no words as she walked away, but she knew what she had to do. She also knew that he may never speak to her again if she did. She loved him too much to stay.

He knew she was gone when he came back. He'd known from the moment his siblings had left maybe before but didn't want to believe it. It was as if Flower and Ghadi had communicated silently from the moment Flower joined them down stairs saying she'd left Delightful to get ready. Get ready for what? He'd left her in his robe for a reason. To chill and make love to her as many times as he could until they wore each other out, collapsing onto each other until neither could think about what they were doing or what lie ahead.

This wasn't on them now. *This was all her,* he thought walking into the silent, bleak expanse of the suite. Gone. Desolate. He wanted to roar. Grief and anger coalesced to cold fury. Part of him wanted to go and drag her back, another wanted to lay waste to everything she held dear. That would mean ripping his own heart out. He already felt hallow. Bereft. How fucking dare she after what they shared? She kept ripping his heart out. She was just cruel.

He walked into the bedroom and saw the neatly folded pajamas and folded stationary atop his robe. Hope sprung in his heart as he opened the note.

FADE,

Twelve years ago I gave you a promise. I was ready to keep that promise then and honestly I had been ready since the moment you came over our house to play video games with Justice when I was in the third grade. Now, if I kept that promise, it would be unfair to both of us. You deserve more than that. I realized as I listened to Flower speak about taking responsibility that I have only been paying lip service to you to get your forgiveness. I am sorry.

Something broke inside of me when Justice died and I have made no effort to repair that. I realized seeing you recover from injuries caused by my actions that I need to work to fix me or I will continue to hurt those I love. What happened to you was wrong and my fault. One day you may want to take your forgiveness back when you have time and space away from me. I will understand if you do.

Love is an action. You have loved me, and my family for years and I took that love for granted. I won't anymore. I won't ask you to wait for me. I won't ask anything other than you to be well and be at peace.

Delightful

"Go to hell, Delightful," he first whispered the words. Then he shouted then crumbling the pages in his hand. Finally, when he could get them through his sobs as he sat down on the edge of the bed. "Go to hell."

ust Relax

"Are the edits ready?" Lovie-Belle asked, standing over her like she was some type of principal.

"Yes, Ms. Lockett," she responded referring to their elementary teacher who'd been stern but taught them to be excellent writers.

Lovie-Belle laughed and waved her off, plopping down beside her. "Just make sure it's done by the morning. They are ready to put this to bed, this should be the last scene you'll have to do."

"It's not a problem truly. I'm lucky they didn't fire me." She grumbled, looking from the notes that had been sent over and back to the computer screen. It wasn't a lot, but it was important that she got it right. When he saw she didn't want any misunderstanding about what she thought of him.

"Are you coming to the screening or are you going to wait for the premier?"

"Your tone is very bossy, little sis." She cut eyes over to her and went back to writing. "If you'll excuse me, then I can get back to work."

"Not bossy — assertive. I get it from my momma." She laughed at her own joke. Then somber her tone softening. "Are you worried that FADE will be there? He won't they sent him the film, and he loved it. This is the only thing he wanted changed."

Delightful dragged her eyes away from her work. "So this is him. He wants his move to New York to include the help he gave to the police to bring Savelle to justice, why?"

"I don't know. He's been giving interviews in the last three months. He's not been shy about telling his side. He's even done pressers with community leaders and ex-gang members, talking about the need to stand up to these vultures that destroy the community. There is nothing wrong with the culture, but there are problems we have to address to move forward. It isn't like he's ever lied about his past, he's just never discussed it and get this, girl. He did an hour on the news with pundits about his depression and how he got help for it. He's started a program for Black men to mentor and help younger guys about dealing with it. When Sadiq told me about it I thought it was just performative, but he's the real deal." Lovie-Belle was leaning in, her eyes sparkling as she spoke.

"Sadiq, huh?' Delightful quirked her eyebrow and watched as her sister's face screwed up with disdain.

"I've told you it's not like that. He wants nothing to do with me like that. Plus, it violates our contract. He'd be liable for a lawsuit." The attitude rolling off her was really remarkable. Delightful knew that her sister did not like to be told no and to see her this disdainful was rare because she was rarely thwarted in her endeavors.

"Well, it's good that the movie is over after the edit this week. Then you can see where it goes," she said in hopes to assuage her.

"Nope. He's always with some leggy model or some such and he's very abrupt with me at times. All business with him. He's cold and aloof. I think when we met he was just being kind because FADE wanted us on board, but now that's all changed. We are only colleagues and he has made sure I know it. He ain't dealing with any little peon director." She laughed, but Delightful knew her sister and heard the hurt. Something had gone on with them. She'd leave it alone and let her work it out. She had her own issues to contend with.

"How's your therapy going?"

"Good." She looked up again at the change of subject. "I'm down to monthly visits now. She's a wonderful listener."

"Awesome," came another voice from the doorway.

"Ohmygod! Miracle, why didn't you have one of us pick you up?" Delightful rose from her floor sitting and rushed over to hug her youngest sister.

"Umm, because I'm grown and can navigate on my own. I know how to call an Uber." She pulled away in a huffed, placing her hand on her curvy hips to glare at her sisters. "We've had this conversation twenty-six now, twenty-seven times."

"Okay, okay," Delightful raised her hands having already lost this argument with her sister several, no, twenty-seven times. She'd let it go for now.

"How's your advocate?" Lovie-Belle asked, patting the area she'd moved to on the sofa, making room for her sister.

"Fired." Miracle moved over to the sink and began washing her hands with meticulous precision. After drying them and rooting around for her unscented moisturizer, she came over to her sister and turned her back.

"Why did you fire your advocate?" Delightful kept her voice neutral, trying to keep her concern banked. Her heart was slamming. Every terrible thing that could happen crossed her mind.

"He fell in love and I felt like it was unfair to keep him when there was no hope of me ever being with him."

"Keep him?" Lovie-Belle clapped her handover her mouth mid-shriek abruptly stopping the deep pressure massage she was giving her sister.

"Girl, you are crazy," Delightful laughed.

"I'm not crazy, I'm Autistic," Miracle deadpanned.

"You just broke poor Josh's, heart," Lovie-Belle laughed.

"He was a fuck-boi and infatuated. What?" Miracle turned to them as Lovie-Belle fell over and Delightful crumbled to the floor.

"D-did you tell him that?" Delightful asked.

"No, that would be rude. It doesn't negate that he was one." Miracle motioned for her sister to get back to the massage.

"Do you want me to do your legs or will that be too much?" Delightful asked, scooting their way, stopping when her sister held up her hand.

"No. I had the Uber to stop two blocks away so I could get my energy out, plus I had my backpack so I got enough input." She closed her eyes, visibly relaxing under her sister's touch.

Silence fell in the room as Lovie-Belle attended to her sister for the next few minutes.

"What are you working on Delightful?" she asked when she moved away grabbing the soft blankets on the sofa and pulling them over her.

"The final edits of this screenplay." She moved back to the

laptop on the floor. "It won't take long and then we can watch movies or whatever you'd like."

"Okay, but I want pizza for dinner." She relaxed under the plush blankets. "Turn the air on, please."

"Okay, I like the way you come here ordering us around," Lovie-Belle chided but got up and did what she asked, going over to the thermostat moving it to the temperature her sister would find the most comfortable.

"I'm here because you begged me, Lovie. You want me to cheer up Delightful since her heart was broken." Her eyes were closed, so she didn't see Delightful's furrowed glare to her sister.

"Oh, really?" Delightful asked, staring daggers at her other sister. "And what else did she say?"

"Miracle, remember you weren't supposed to say anything?' Lovie-Belle rushed in.

"Do you know how ridiculous you sound when you ask me to keep a secret then tell me I need to tell you all everything for my safety?" She sat up, looking between the both of them. "Please be consistent."

"Okay," they answered together, gazes hot with anger at each other.

"If you're going to fight, I won't stay. We're supposed to love each other, remember? Delightful, Lovie called because she loves you and was concerned. Lovie, you know I will tell it. How many times has mommy said that?" she smiled hopefully at them.

They shook their heads and gave her a rueful smile.

"Okay, let me get done and we will watch Black Panther."

"Whoop-whoop!" Miracle cheered at hearing one of her favorite movie, "How about something with Kris Kryrikos?"

"Why am I not surprised?" Lovie-Belle muttered. "You should come to the premiere of the movie, they sent out invitations, and he's on the list. You know he got his start doing movies with the Al Rasheed brothers."

"Really?" Miracle eyes lit up. Her sisters smiled, willing to do anything to make her happy. "I will go if Delightful goes. Lovie you're a butterfly and will be flitting all over the place. Delightful can be my support person. Will you?"

"You know I absolutely will." Delightful answered, having no intention of going to the premier until that very moment. She didn't want to mar FADE's night. She'd not had any contact with him in time she'd left him the suite in Birmingham and she doubted if he ever wanted to see her again. She'd hesitated, though she longed to contact Flower to ask how he was since she knew he'd gone back to New York. She'd stayed off social media, which is why everything Lovie-Belle had said was news to her. She was happy that he was finding his way, even if it was without her. She knew he'd shine without her. He'd already proven that. She had needed to see if she could live her life without her sole motivation — her vendetta. Had she thrived? She'd written two projects and got them both optioned. Her work had not suffered, but her heart was in shreds. She felt hallowed out. Numb. As if part of her had been amputated. Ripped away and cast into the sea. The time they'd spent together ruined her for all others. She saw now that it had not only been Justice's death that she grieved. Those twelve years she had also missed FADE. She'd just put all her energy in her vendetta and her pursuit of success. Now, after months of therapy, she now realized the truth of what she'd done to them both.

"So FADE broke your heart?" Miracle asked. After they watched both movies and Lovie-Belle was asleep.

"No, it was me who hurt him," she said to her sister. As

she gathered up all the used snack bags and containers and threw them in the trash.

"So what now? Are you going to apologize?" Miracle had come to the counter separating the eat-in kitchen and the living room and cupped her chin in her hand, watching Delightful with steady determination.

"I have and he forgave me but there is a lot I did that is probably not worthy of forgiveness." Delightful braved through the statement that had been her mantra. She knew what she wanted, but she had no right to demand anything from him. She was doing the work on herself and from Lovie-Belle's revelations it seemed he had too. And his conclusion must be that he was better off without her. It had been six months. He'd gotten his company back together and his career was back on the upswing. All on his own and there was nothing people loved more than a comeback and he was the guy who had done it. A bootstrapper. The American Dream on steroids. Having her in his life would be nothing but an aggravation he probably didn't need and definitely didn't want.

"Well, if he forgave you maybe y'all can be friends, now?" Delightful knew that her sister could still be innocent about some things, so she said. "You know how Josh didn't want to be just friends? Well, FADE and I can't just be friends anymore either."

"Because you love him with all your heart." Her eyes were shinning with unshed tears and Delightful could have kicked herself knowing how much empathy her sister had for others.

"Yep," she deliberately put an upbeat note in her voice. "And that's okay, Miracle. There are plenty of people I love with all my heart that I don't get to see all the time. You being one."

She hugged her.

"Yeah, but FADE is different for you," her voice sounded so sad, that it took everything for Delightful not to cry because then they be in a bonafide cry-fest and wake Lovie-Belle who had fallen asleep and a six AM call time.

"I promise I'm okay," she assured her patting her on the back.

"What about FADE?" She whimpered into her shoulder.

"FADE is fine.'

"He can't be, Delightful. He lost Justice who was his friend soulmate and now you, his love soulmate how can either of you ever be fine?" She then hugged her so hard Delightful could do nothing but try to hold on to the thread of control she had remaining or just crumble.

As darkness surrounded, she looked at her phone. She couldn't help but stare at the message. She typed her finger on the edge. She knew he maybe was up even at two AM. He was a creative and like her kept late hours.

DELIGHTFUL: Hey

FADE:...

FADE:...

Delightful: Lovie-Belle asked about the premiere and Miracle wants to go with me as her support person. I didn't want the night to be awkward for anyone. I wanted to give you a head's up.

FADE:...

FADE: I'd love to have Miracle there.

COLD-BLOODED, she thought. Okay, she'd go as Miracle's support person and stay out of his way. He'd moved on, that was obvious, so she needed to do the same. How she would navigate Ghadi and Flower, she had no idea. She was sure them seeing her with Miracle would be enough to let them know that she was not out for their brother again. She wouldn't have time anyway because crowds were never Miracle's strength. They tended to overwhelm her with sensory input. Too many smells, unfamiliar tones of voices and people invading her space. They would probably need to get there early and leave as soon as the film was over to avoid the crush of people. They would probably be nowhere near FADE and his entourage. Which was a good thing since some of the antics of his friends and hangers on would be too much for Miracle and she definitely didn't want to be around him if he had a date. She'd be crushed. She'd left him, so what could she say? She told him she couldn't ask him to wait, and why should he?

Lovie-Belle would have told her if he was seeing someone else, yet the premier was a huge deal. She doubted he'd show up with no one on his arm.

Putting the phone away, she snuggled into her covers. Her nose stung. Her heart hurt. She had no one to blame but herself for the love she squandered. Like most nights since she left him, she cried herself to sleep.

J ust Lonely

"WHY ARE you looking at your phone?" FADE tucked his phone in his pocket and turned to his youngest sister, Willow. "Are they ready for me?"

"Almost," she quirked an eyebrow at him. "Are you seriously not going to tell me?" she huffed. "It better not be one of those side-chicks, video vixens or thots that are always trying to get with you."

"You are all up in my business, little girl." He wrinkled his nose at her and stood looking at his reflection in the green room mirror.

"Says the guy who makes me and Flower's life all his business," she laughed like ha-ha-ha in his face.

"Not anymore," he muttered.

"That's because she won't tell you. Don't worry if it was something detrimental she'd have told me and mom and she's hit her stride now so leave her alone. That beard looks good on you, by the way." She patted him on his back, but he found no solace in that. He'd been powerless when his sister needed him most, and that did not sit well with him at all.

"A minor change is all it takes to revamp an image or so I've been told by Flower." He peered at his reflection. He looked mature, as if he'd put away childish things. Debonair was what his mother said when she got a look at him. He immediately pushed down the feeling of wanting to know what Delightful thought.

"I still want to know what went down." He smacked his hand on the counter, causing her to jump.

"And that right there is why you won't know. You can't go killing everyone you think has wronged someone you love. Now you have to field some crazy questions today, I hope you're ready." She got the lint brush and ran it across his shoulders.

"I have people for that," he muttered.

"Flower sent me because she and Ghadi have that meeting with the Mc2 people to solidify the deal for the IPO. And it's not like I had anything else to do, I'm on hiatus." She reminded him double-checking to make sure everything was nipped and tucked the way he needed it to be.

"I appreciate everything you have sacrificed for us, Willow. I hate that you came off tour with your company to take care of Flower and me."

"Nonsense. That's what family does." She tossed the lint brush on the counter causing a clattering sound and sat in the seat he'd just vacated and started swiveling from side to side. "You want to know something?"

"What?"

"I hated dancing with them. They were too rigid. Too rote. I need more creativity in my life. There are so may companies here. I was their lead dancer. I can dance for any company I choose now that I've made a name for myself. I may just stay home til my contract runs out." She shrugged.

"I thought you were happy with them. You traveled all over the world…" he trailed off at the revelation as she shook her head 'No'.

"Nope. Nopity, nope, nope. Traveling is awesome but not with that crew. I was over it after the first tour. They were too cut-throat. You think the rap game is vicious just try out for prima ballerina for Swan Lake. Those little ninety-five pounders will cut your throat." He chuckled watching her imitate slitting her throat.

"Well, I know mom and dad missed you."

"They miss you now." She quirked an eyebrow at him. "You haven't been to Sunday dinner in a while."

"I'm coming Sunday."

"Ghadi, said you'd say that." Again the eyebrow he sighed, and she mocked him.

"You keep that up and I am going to lock you in a trunk," he threatened.

"There aren't any here," she teased.

"It's a tv studio I'm sure they have one somewhere." He spun her around for emphasis.

"Whee," she laughed. "Again. Again."

A knock came at the door. "Five minutes, Mr. Carrington."

They looked at each other, sheepish expressions spread across their faces.

"So unprofessional," he chided. "Flower will be livid if she hears about this."

"Not at you. I was supposed to be the one keeping you in line, remember?" she grumbled. "Give the PA an autograph or something to keep him quiet."

"This barely registers on their radar. Think of all the

people he's probably caught having sex in here. In that chair, even."

"Ew," she squealed and jumped up.

"I'm sure they cleaned it," He laughed as they headed to the door. "Or wiped it down with a dirty rag." He winked at her shiver, knowing she was a germaphobe.

"So FADE you have this movie coming out, Just Forever; new artist signing up to your label with the IPO back on track. How does it feel your being on the comeback?" Jessica the entrainment reporter cheesed at him with a thousand watt smile. She was a former Miss America, Teen USA or whatever, but he could tell she was thirsting for more. He liked when people were hungry for success it either made them ruthless or reckless sometimes both but you could always use it to your advantage.

"It feels great. I'm always grateful to my fans for believing in me," he smiled back at her keeping his tone mild. Showing any type of emotion was always a mistake. It was better to seem aloof than to be depicted as a raging maniac. Not that this interview would be anything other than a puff piece. Flower had seen to that.

"Hm," she kind of tilted her in the manner that every reported did to imitate Barbara Walters before she cut some-one's throat. Reckless it was then. "Your fans seem to still be grumbling about this snitch moniker you've embrace. You've gone around defending your actions of twelve years ago as if you were some type of folk hero," she fake chuckled. "They say you broke the code."

He shrugged, "I don't know what type of code you are speaking of. My code, my integrity and the way I was raised say take care of your people, help your community and that's what I have always done and shall continue to do." He kept his tone low but allowed enough passion to bleed through. He had months of training and had done enough interviews in print, live and online at this point that he could take on all comers.

"Last question." She paused for dramatic emphasis. "Your former associate, Mr. Giano Savelle…"

"He was not my associate. I've never met him but finish your question." He lifted his hand in her direction in the most unbothered way possible, though rage was slowly building inside of him at even the mention of the man's name who caused his friend's death.

"Mr. Savelle was found murdered in his prison cell," she said with such relish. The woman was almost bouncing from her seat in her excitement in what she thought was a gotcha interview.

He quirked his eyebrow, waiting for her to finish.

"You don't have anything to say about this?" She tilted her head in the caricature of a serious journalist again.

"No. Why would I?" He answered her question with one of his own. This was bordering on ridiculous and he was done playing.

"Mr. Savelle was murdered…"

"How?"

"Hm." She rifled through from what he could see were blank notes then looked to him. "He was hanged."

"Then I would look to his cellmate." He knew for a fact that Savelle didn't have one or he'd have been dead years ago.

"He was alone at the time," she responded, her lips all but disappearing under her frown of disappointment. Had she been cleverer and less obvious it may have worked, but no. Now she would have to contend with an interview of her looking mean spirited and not quite bright.

"Sounds like a suicide to me," he said then canted his head to let the audience get a full picture of himself in the camera without breaking the fourth wall. He knew it would go viral before he left the studio."Prayers to the family. I know what it's like to lose someone you love. I would also like to speak about my mental health initiatives for young men."

* * *

"SHE PLAYED HERSELF," Willow said as they were in the car on the way back to Creative Chaos.

"Yeah," FADE murmured, scrolling through his news feed for any information on the Savalle suicide. Dread crept up his spine. A niggling feeling he couldn't shake the whole ride back to the glass mid-city high-rise that housed their company.

It rode him from the time he got out of the car all the way to the top floor of the building that contained his office and the boardroom.

When he got there Flower and Ghadi were already there and to his surprise the Al Rasheed brothers.

"Surprise, surprise," he said to them shaking hands and slapping backs all around.

"What brings you to town?"

"The premier," Hasan said. "We needed to sit down with Flower and go over security. Nothing happens without her express say so." He winked at her but FADE could tell he was a little annoyed.

He was not the type of man to be maneuvered and bossed around by a woman. They were in for a rude wakening if they thought to get anything other than that from Flower. Especially now. She was like a whirlwind of intention and action since she came back from Birmingham and Japan. There was a fire under her like never before and she had worked tirelessly to right the ship.

"Great news," she stood up at the head of the conference

table. "Mc2 has agreed to come on broad with minimal oversight into our day to day and shepherd us into the IPO. They will look at our financials which are sound then after a review we will be good to go. They are going to be very thorough but we knew that going in. You have done everything we needed you to do to revamp your image and today that hit job and the way you handle it was a superb demonstration of your sound business mind and your philanthropic spirit. I'm proud of you, big brother. You looked the part of a mogul and you acted like one."

To say he basked in her smile would be an understatement. His sister had done everything she could to help him get his life back. Pushing her dream aside until he was ready to stand on his own again.

He held out his arms to her, and she practically ran to them. "I love you," he whispered in her ear. "I love you back, FADE," her muffled response against his heart was everything. They had been through so much.

"Okay," he clapped his hands, stepping from big brother to CEO mode. "Let's hear this security plan."

"These are the VIPs," Sadiq said, going over the list of high-powered Hollywood stars, executives and music industry people who'd received a personal invitation to come the premier.

"Wait a fricking minute, what is this name doing on the list?" Ghadi piped up. FADE turned to look at his brother, knowing exactly what he was referring to.

"She wrote the movie," Sadiq calmly reminded everyone. "She did everything that was asked of her and more. I see no reason to exclude her."

"It will take away from FADE's night. People will start whispering again." Ghadi slapped the table in disgust.

"That is a moot point. Your brother has set the record straight on that issue. She will not be in the main entourage but escorting her younger sister who needs help to navigate the space." Hasan rubbed the bridge of his nose, supporting the decision.

"Did you agree to this FADE?"

"Yes." He steepled his fingers and swiveled his chair toward his siblings. "It's fine. It's over. There will be more than one ex there, this is business. To exclude her is mean spirited and unprofessional. She wrote the movie, man."

"And almost got you killed over some stupid ass vendetta."

"That too," Flower murmured. "FADE is right though. Now, let's move on to the after party." She skipped to the next screen, going over the various weak spots and how she planned to reinforce the security team.

"Excellent job, Flower," he said, as the others nodded as they concluded the meeting nearly an hour later.

She smiled and gathered her things. "I promised Willow dinner at my place you're all invited," she said to the men as she headed to the door.

"Stop walking so fast if you want us to join you."

"Hush, dinner is later. Around eight is good for everyone?"

She smiled at the chorus of yeses and headed out. Feeding people was an expression of love from Flower as passed down from generations of their family. Being farmers in Alabama their ancestors had little else but what they did have whether it was part of a crop or sweet potato pie they shared it. So, if they cooked for you, they cared for you. He looked forward to whatever she had in store for them later.

"Savelle is dead." He turned to the men still gathered around the table.

"Good," Ghadi said with relish dripping from the word.

"We saw that." Sadiq's face was wiped clear of all emotion. So was Hasan's who finally let his real self shine through now that the women were gone. He'd never shown his true face to anyone but FADE and his brother. Many people mistook his charm and charisma for kindness, and that is where they went wrong. He was by far the most dangerous of the twin Al Rasheed brothers.

"It was more than he deserved." Hasan didn't blink, smile or give any indication that he was bothered by any of it at all.

"They are going to say I did it." FADE kept his tone level, though anger licked at him.

"Good, maybe next time folks will think twice before trying to fuck with us," Ghadi ground out.

"I've just barely got my name back. What are the Mc2 people going to think if they feel like I just go around having people killed?"

"That they better not wrong you. Look, sometimes a message has to be sent. I only wish we were the ones to send it." Sadiq raised his hand in a "what can you do" motion.

"This wasn't...?" FADE asked into the room at large.

They all shook their heads.

"Ghad?" he asked again for confirmation.

"He was too secure for anyone to get to him." Hasan's frustration was evident in his voice.

"So it wasn't for lack of trying?" FADE gave a hollow laugh to the room at large. "You just couldn't get to him."

Shaking his head, he walked over to the floor to ceiling windows and looked out. "Incredible."

"Something like this can't go unanswered. You'd look like a chump," Ghadi told him matter-of-factly.

"You mean more of one. You already think I'm one over Delightful." FADE looked over his shoulder at his brother.

"That's different. Relationships are not the streets. Savelle needed to be seen to. Whoever did it." Ghadi shrugged. "Did you a favor because he was never going to stop until you were dead."

"They say it was suicide but I know those guards can make anything look like a suicide and since he got so many life sentences he has to be buried on the prison burial ground."

"Well, what done is done my friend. Your story is the only one that counts now and it will play across every screen in the country in a few short days." Sadiq assured him with cold alacrity.

ust See

"THIS IS SO OUTSTANDING. Isn't it outstanding? I love it." Delightful heard her sister who was never impressed about anything squee about everything that had to do with the *Just Forever* premier. Everyone was dressed in white in honor of FADE's signature look. He was known for preferring a blindingly white on white ensemble for everything. The theme for the entire space was white on white and bling. The red carpet was a white carpet, the velvet ropes were white, and everyone from the attendants to the guests were all dressed in white.

Every celebrity and insta-famous person was there. It rivaled the Creative Chaos Oscar party that happened what seemed like a lifetime ago. This venue was open to nearly every relevant of hip hop artist, old and new. There were the godfathers of hip hop, the DJ's, radio host, the scholars, video directors, vixens, mavens and aspiring artists all there to see the movie of the most successful rap artist of their time. The culture came to support one of their own being feted like never before.

FADE had done so much over the past few months to rehabilitate his image as well as forge an alternative path for himself. He'd made a clean break away from the snitch stigma proving that all it took was someone with enough power and force behind their name to change the narrative. That was the only way to get those communities that were suffering back, he argued. Stop giving a pass to the very people preying on you. They don't deserve your loyalty. It would probably still take more than him, but him being unapologetic about it went a long way to re-establish his street cred.

"Where are we sitting?" Miracle asked, brimming with excitement.

"I don't know. The attendant will lead us to the correct area." She took her sister's hand and walked over to the attendant.

"Miracle and Delightful Howard," she told the attendant who nodded and looked down the guest the list. He called over an usher who led them to the VIP reception area.

There were a lot of people but nowhere near the number that would be there in an hour when FADE and his entourage probably came, which would include Lovie-Belle and the Al Rasheed brothers.

She led her sister over to the bar and got herself a gin and tonic and Miracle flavored water.

Just as they sipped on the cold beverages a commotion erupted at the entrance of the lounge. Her heart stopped as she turned to look, but only a little because Miracle was cutting the circulation to her fingers from gripping them so hard.

"Kristantinos," Miracle whispered, her voice hushed in awe. "Jeeze Louise."

"Indeed." She knew he was a living, breathing person, but she too was a little star struck. He was six-foot-five and all rippling muscle. The biggest star in the world had his hair cut in a buzz cut and a kilowatt smile that could have panties dropping for miles.

Josh couldn't get it, but looking at her sister now, she knew that Kristantinos "The Kronic" Kryrikos could get it on steroids.

As if feeling that vibe, his eyes lifted and met her sister's and Delightful could have sworn it felt like she'd gotten the residue strike of whatever energy infused Miracle from that look.

"Ohmygoodness, he's coming this way." Miracle whispered, taking a drink of her water.

"Breathe, don't worry." She assured her easing her numb hand loose and holding her by the waist instead like it was a causal hug but she was applying deep pressure to ground her.

"Hi," his voice was like smooth velvet, "I'm Kris." He smiled down at them — no, correction at Miracle introducing himself.

"I'm Delightful and this is my sister, Miracle." Please don't let him be a jerk. She prayed as she heard Miracle introduce herself. A lot of times people didn't realize she was neurodivergent until she spoke or engaged in conversation but if he noticed it didn't matter because he his eyes warmed more as they conversed.

After Miracle eased away Delightful dropped her hand as her sister as she often did no longer needed her support once she got used to the environment she was in. She was so engrossed in watching the sheer happiness on her sister's face that she forgot about the time.

She heard the swell before she saw it. She longed to tear

Miracle away and find a nice cubby hole to hide, but found she could not be that selfish nor that much of a coward. Her mother would be so disappointed if she knew those thoughts had crossed her mind. She didn't raise cowards, she often said whenever they were faced with adversity, and they definitely were never allowed to quit.

She watched as person after person came in, her heart lurching with each new arrival. There was an area that had been cornered off for the entourage and special guests of FADE and the Al Rasheed brothers. She could hear the cheers and well wishes. Trepidation slithered through her. Her throat was tight and she could feel perspiration trickling down her back. Then first the Al Rasheed brothers came in along with Lovie-Bell in a white linen couture wrap dress that clung to every curve. She noticed that Sadiq had a hand on the small of her sister's back and wore an expression that threaten to slice any man who even looked her sister's way. Okay, then.

The Carrington family followed with heavy security that swallowed Flower's petite form, but she got a clear look at Ghadi as they were shepherded to the VIP area situated up a flight of steps to the left of them. Unfortunately, he got a clear look at her and it was obvious from his expression that he still had no love for her. She met his glare unflinchingly. His eyes narrowed before he finally turned to go into the area.

The crowd gave way like the Red Sea when FADE came in and he looked like a mother-fucking god. He wore white from head to toe but it held a little sheen that said this was posh. It was as if his tailor had poured him into that suit. She could see the barest outline of his dick and her heart fluttered, and her core tightened, remembering, longing. Not to mention the silk shirt he had on left a mouthwatering display of chiseled chest. The two thin platinum chains sparkled when the light hit them. It was an enticement to be perfectly honest she remembered how they felt when they brushed her nipples when he loomed over her giving her the most exquisite pleasure she'd ever experienced.

She swallowed against the thought as the motion of them stopped. He'd stopped, she saw as she looked up and saw that his eyes were trained on her. His gaze was cool and assessing as his eyes raked her from head to toe. She was aware for the first time of the form fitting jumpsuit that she'd worn that hugged every ounce of her. She couldn't get a credit card between her and the material. She loved it the moment she'd seen it and secretly wanted him to notice her in it. He did, and she could tell from where she stood that his eyes smoldered. That wasn't enough to get him to come over or acknowledge her though. He swung away when tapped on the shoulder by his security team and went in the direction of the rest of the entourage. She stood for a long time watching him go, knowing she looked like a lovesick idiot. There were probably even now hidden paparazzi plants in the throng who'd taken pictures of her obvious display. Until now no one had been able to confirm their connection or prove they'd had a brief love affair, but her reaction to him was enough to give life to the rumors again.

She turned back to the bar. "Another gin and tonic, please."

The bartender nodded, and she took a sip, watching as her baby sister and the biggest star in the world had their heads together like they were best friends.

"Excuse me Mr. Kyrikos, Mr. Al Rasheed has requested that you join them in the VIP lounge."

"I thought this was the VIP lounge." Kris, she had to keep reminding herself not to use the moniker, "the Kronic" turned to the guy puzzled.

"The above area is for exclusive guest requiring a certain amount of security," the guy explained.

Kris took this all in and nodded. "Good. I'm bringing my two friends here along with me."

"I'm sorry sir we allow only those already vetted by security in the lounge," he hedged, his eyes darting to her in such a way that she knew he'd been expressly told to keep her away from FADE. They probably had been given her picture.

"This is the woman who wrote the film, Delightful Howard," he said, then nodded toward Miracle. "This is her sister. If anyone says anything to you, then just tell them I pushed past you and wouldn't listen. Ladies?" He held his hands out, his eyes softening toward Miracle, who accepted with a shy smile. Delightful hurried to put down her glass and grasped his other offered hand. What was happening? Kept reverberating in her mind as she walked arm in arm with the biggest star on the planet with Miracle on the other side.

Up the stairs they went and through the double doors as if the security meant nothing. Which it obviously didn't when the person was a human movie franchise coming through the door.

"The Kronic has arrived," Kris hailed bringing all the attention to them making Delightful visibly cringe, "And I have the lovely Delightful and the beautiful Miracle with me." She should have been mad, but the worshipful tone his voice took on when he mentioned her sister made her forgive him.

"Okay, we should just go hang out back there, Miracle since our seats aren't up here."

"I'll make sure you guys have a seat." He looked around to call another attendant, but she stopped him. "No, it's okay just see after Miracle. Are you okay with that Miracle?"

"Sure. Lovie-Belle said that FADE said I could sit up here, but I just didn't want to leave you alone."

She nodded her mind a whole lot of "wow" right now thinking her baby sister had taken pity on her so she wouldn't be left alone or not come to see the movie she'd written.

She made her way to the back of the room. She looked around and noticed that the lounge had the best view in the house. The chairs were all in a huge semi-circle facing the screen, there were two tiered rows so no one would be in another person's way. The back area had a bar and buffet with attendants.

She saw that Kris had led Miracle to an end chair and sat on the floor beside her. An attendant rushed over with a folding chair, but the gesture still impressed her. People spoke of his kindness, but to see it in action was marvelous. He was the real deal.

"I'm glad you came." She jumped, startled to see Flower had come up beside her.

"I'm very surprised to hear you say that." She turned fully to face her. "Since you were the one who insisted I never see FADE again."

"I did not but I won't apologize for telling you to get yourself together before you end up hurting him again." Flower put her hands on her hips like a little general. *FADE and Ghadi were at fault for letting this little hellion get crazed with power,* she thought. She just ran around regulating like a miniature Olivia Pope or something.

"If that's the way you see it." Delightful nodded and kept her voice low. She didn't need to make a scene, and she was at a disadvantage. Flower held all the power here, all five-feet-two of her in Louboutins. She was his sister and the boss at events like this. "I see he's doing just fine, so you were obviously right about me leaving him alone."

It hurt her to say it, but other than that look, he'd not given her any indication that he wanted her. There was a big difference between wanting a person for sex and wanting them to have a significant presence in your life.

She knew what leaving him could mean, and she did it. For him. Part of her wanted to shout and rail at Flower, but there was nothing she could do when the woman was right. She'd been nothing but toxic the moment she'd come back into his life. The one selfless thing she'd ever done was leave him to heal without her. She didn't want him to think he owed Justice anything more. He never did in the first place. Now maybe he could see that. Now when his emotions for her weren't tied up in promises he made as a seventeen-year-old kid, would he still choose her? If tonight was any sign, she had her answer.

"Well, look who the cat dragged in." She turned to the good-humored voice of Lyric, her brother's former girlfriend.

"Wow, Lyric, you look amazing as usual." She hugged the woman to her. Seeing her was always bittersweet.

"I know, right?" The super star preened as she did a slow turn so they could check out her outfit, which was sure to be on every fashion blog come tomorrow. She also had on a jumpsuit, but the pants were tied like harem pants and every seam had crystal embellishments. She was stunning, her skin sparkled with diamond dust that accentuated the dark hues. She always embraced her curves and sex positivity. She was both loved and reviled for her frankness about her life and displayed it in her art unapologetically.

Delightful knew that Justice would have been proud of the woman the girl he'd loved since six grade had become. He would have cheered her on with unrestrained pride.

When Lyric finished her turn, they all laughed at her antics.

"Splendid," Flower smiled, her eyes glowing with warmth. "I think FADE is saving the seat beside him for you." She nodded toward the center of the first row. Delightful couldn't resist looking in that direction and see him now talking to his mother who was to his right and yes, there was an empty seat by him.

"I need food first," Lyric said, moving past them.

"You better hurry the movie start in five minutes," Flowered warned, looking at her watch. No smart watch for her but a vintage Longines graced her thin wrist before she looked back up to her again. "You did a brave thing, Delightful. That's what I came over her to say. I'm proud of you for that and what it meant for my brother. He has his life back now. After tonight he will be back on top."

She looked back down where FADE sat watching as Lyric moved to sit beside him. They allowed the press to take pictures of them before being ushered out with promises of interviews later.

"He won't be happy without you though." She didn't bother to turn and watch Flower walk away because whatever Lyric said had FADE looking over his shoulder at her.

The lights dimmed, but not before she felt the heat of his glare. She wanted to shrink into the wall and disappear. That look spoke of a promise of dark things. Things she'd craved. Things that would leave her longing for him forever if he chose not to stay.

ust Us

"So you've decided to stop running?" The movie was almost over and Delightful tore her eyes away from the screen to look at him. She'd watched him more than the movie. She knew she would find herself face to face with him. It wasn't until he'd gotten up to talk to some of the critics assembled that she allowed herself to focus on what they had created. The film was magnificent. It was a poignant portrayal of the artist and the man. FADE was shown as he was — a hero to many and reviled by some. He was flawed and fascinating. The depiction would rival any Oscar winning performance and would probably earn the entire team a golden statue.

"I'm not the one who refused to answer my texts last night." She pressed her lips together to shut off the words that wanted to spill forth. Not the time nor the place to have it out over their past. Plus, she sounded petty when he'd allowed both Miracle and her to come.

"I didn't leave you before what could have been an epic Netflix binge session topped with more awesome sex." He put his arm up, partly shielding, partly caging her. She inhaled his scent. He smelled delectable. His wrist was exposed and the tendons there flexed and she wanted to sink her teeth into that space.

She nodded. What else could she do? There was no denying his words. At least he was not attempting to eviscerate her before the entire entourage. Because that would go bad for them both. She wasn't about to be publicly humiliated.

"You're looking stunning." His eyes looked like he wanted to eat her up. She would let him. She would let him do anything if it meant she'd get a chance to touch him once again. She shouldn't she knew that. She was setting herself up for an enormous heart shattering disappointment.

"You're looking pretty fantastic yourself," she kept her voice light and unbothered. Not taking anything too seriously would probably be the only what she didn't come away from this situation a crippling heap of tears. She felt a visceral reaction with that thought. That was who she had been the first few months she'd left him in the suite. Doing nothing but keeping her therapy appointments and working on her projects. Her work had been what had seen her through those darkest times.

Staying off social media had helped, but there were always trickles of information finding their way to her. The various women he'd taken up with. All of them models or the usual brand of actress. She did her best to ignore it, but it grated all the same. Then she would remind herself that she had no claim on him. She had walked away from any right to him.

"I'm surprised you don't have a date. I thought you and Angelica Rose were all hot for each other." She just couldn't help herself, it seemed, she thought, sounding pathetic and jealous.

The corner of his mouth kicked up. He blinked slowly, assessing her in a silence that made her feel like she'd been split wide open in the scorching Alabama sun.

"Is that how you see me?" He nodded his head toward the movie screen. Dread crept up. She'd taken liberties. She wanted people to see the person she now knew him to be. Maybe it didn't totally jive with what he wanted the public to know.

"I thought you saw the dailies? We could have changed it if there was something you didn't want shown," she hedged.

"I don't like to micro-manage. I wanted to see it for the first time with mom and dad. I wanted my response to be genuine when I did the shows and interviews afterwards." He shrugged.

"I wanted people to see some of the good that you've done. I think kids need to know that you got your degree in music and that education matters. I think folks need to know about your support for the military and how your dad was a hero with a Purple Heart. I-I know how private you are about all of those things but it painted a fuller picture of your life and some of the things that motivated you. Your fame didn't happen because of Justice's death, but despite it. You were right to not want it in there. I insisted then I realized that I was making the story about him and not you. That was unfair of me and I apologize." Her hand twisted over and over like she'd been called to the principal's office as she waited for his response. His jaw ticked. He swallowed as he seamed to struggle with some emotion unknown to her.

"I'm not that heroic. It was good cinema." His tone was low, but the look in his eyes conveyed so much more. He was giving her hope. She dare not grasp it. To give it a name and then see it fall apart would be her undoing. She tried to hold on to the affirmations. She tried to fight back the fear that ate at her and the what could have been recriminations if she'd only trusted just once and not fucked it all up. This would not do. Nope. She needed to leave, to get away from him and the temptation he presented. She ducked under his arm and skated around him, heading for the nearest exit.

"Twelve years…" She stopped hearing his voice over the loudspeakers, "so many tears. So many fears. Then I saw you for the first time in twelve years. I'm never letting you go. No matter how many times you walk out that door. I will be here waiting. Anticipating, longing for you."

Tears swam in her eyes as she heard the song that he was working out the beat of the first night they made love.

"Now that I have you, I'm never leaving you, You don't have to run anymore, I'm your home, you never have to be alone, you have a home. After twelves years, so many tears, so many fears, I'm here waiting, anticipating, longing for you."

She turned back to him. Her heart was thudding. It was the only thing she could hear. She could barely see his face, but she saw him move her way.

FADE ASKED himself what the hell he was doing when he caught up with her but deliberately held back a few feet. She looked like a deer caught in the headlights hearing that song. Nobody wanted it in the film. Sadiq, Hasan even Lovie-Belle said it was too raw. It was too revealing, they said. He realized as he approached her, he probably always knew why he insisted they keep it. For this very reason — for her to finally see.

It didn't matter if she didn't come to the movie premier

or saw it in video at some point she would hear this song and know without a doubt how he felt. How he fucking ached. How much she was loved. He knew she was going to run again. She wasn't ready to face what they could be, what she could possibly lose.

"You wrote this song for me."

"You wrote this movie for me." He dipped down to look in her eyes. He saw her fear and her hope.

"I'm done waiting Didi," he said watching her brush tears out of her eyes. He watched her finally walk over to him and look up at him.

"I not fucking running anymore, FADE."

"Come home with me." He wasn't asking.

ust Keep Me

DELIGHTFUL TOOK A DEEP, shaky breath. She could not believe she was coming to FADE's penthouse that was in a mid-city high-rise. Never dreamed after what happened between them he'd allow her near him, let alone invite her back to his home. She knew from everything she'd read and all the interviews she done. No one entered his sanctuary.

The place looked like a palace in the sky. No brash displays of toxic masculinity here. Any woman would find comfort in his home. Linen, vegan leather and glass were the main decorative elements.

There were crystal and quartz tables and a whole wall of windows facing the city.

"Do you like it?' he asked in her ear. They'd not touched, not once since he told her she was coming home with him. She was nervous. Anticipation cloaked every movement. She knew trembled with it. The lightest brush of his touch would be her undoing. He was setting out to punish or pleasure. He probably planned both. Her breath caught a little at the thought. She wanted that and more. She would present her body before him as an offering to his every desire. He'd given her no indication despite the heated looks here and there.

"It's beautiful. Did Flower help you decorate this place?" She turned and followed him deeper into the space.

"No," he chuckled. "She has great taste, but she has more a books and bohemian vibe. Clean lines and cut glass are my speed. Flower likes plush." He poured them two fingers each of Laugavalin.

She drank the whiskey, looking at him over the rim. His eyes never left hers as they sipped.

His lips on the glass had her mind tracking back to the way they felt on her body. Her breath clouded the glass. She licked the rim, wishing it was him. His eyes narrowed as he watched.

He tossed the rest back.

"You wasted it." She murmured.

"I have better uses for it." He put the glass down on the other side of the quartz counter and turned towards her. He grabbed her by her waist and pulled her to him. His lips tasted smoky, a hint of vanilla, sherry and peat. His tongue plunged, taking complete possession of her. She reveled in the command he took, loving the way he gripped her by the back of her head as he took her mouth again and again. She couldn't shift or move to her left or right. She had to take him. No retreat. Only surrender. No fucking running. He wanted her mouth, he could have it. He wanted her body, he could have it.

"I want you so fucking bad," he growled in her ear.

His beard scraped her but it was so soft that she wanted to nuzzle him. He rubbed down the side of her face and neck, eliciting all types of tingly sensations that made her skin prickle.

"Can I have you, Didi? Like I want?" He pulled back to look in her eyes.

She swallowed, knowing that he was going to put her through her paces just based on the ask alone.

"Nothing that you don't want," he murmured, his eyes blazingly hard.

He was so close she could feel how hard his dick was. She wanted him. "I want you." She tipped her mouth for him to take again.

He slow walked her until her back was to the counter. She gasped when he lifted her placing her on the counter and stood between them pressing her knees farther apart spreading them wide.

Her pussy was pressed tightly against the linen. She could feel her own wetness against the material. He rubbed the inside of her legs, beginning at her knees with a slow drag until his fingers met at the apex of her thighs.

"You're so fucking wet. Why is your pussy so wet Didi?" He looked down at her as he touched her, rubbing his fingers over the material in maddening swirls. She didn't try to hide her moans.

"Where are you panties?" he growled, concentrating his fingers on her clit, stroking with barely there touches.

"I can't wear them with this outfit." His fingers stopped at her words.

"So all night you've been sashaying this ass — my ass around with no panties?" He quirked his eyebrow as he reached around and gripped her plump cheeks.

She bit her bottom lip and nodded.

"And had the nerve to have nothing covering you but this thin ass material. Look at how soaked it is. I can see your sweet little pussy begging for me to touch it, kiss it." He shook his head sadly. His gaze crawling slowly from her center to her eyes, then back again.

He reached behind her and unzipped the jumpsuit. Unsnapped it just above the cut-out that left her back bare. "No bra either," he mused, sounding ominous and sexy. If it were possible, her body responded more. Her nipples budded and hardened more when the cool air hit them as he pulled the bodice down over her shoulders, leaving her bare to him.

"Up," he ordered as he pulled the pants along with the top down and off lying it over one of the bar stools.

"Let me see how much you want me." He gently urged her legs open, spreading them wide for him.

He pressed his hand on her tummy. She rested on her elbows and watched him as his fingers moved lower and lower still. He caressed the sides, slicking wetness allover her. He delved into the center with one long finger swirling around only to push deeper then retreat. She panted, canting her hips toward him, chasing the sensations he was evoking, meeting each thrust of his fingers. She felt so close. She cried out when he withdrew and screamed his name when he covered her with his mouth as his tongue did tortuous maddening things. She opened herself further, completely surrendering to him. She was cresting when his fingers entered her again, taking her over the brink as he thrust inside, pressing against her G-spot. The pleasure made her see stars against tightly shut eyelids as her essence drench his hands. She watched through dazed eyes as he sucked them clean before placing gentle kisses on her thighs.

He ripped his shirt over his head. She marveled at the chiseled planes of his chest. He was magnificent. He looked completely recovered from his ordeal. The only signs were the faint lines where his incisions were and she could see the bullet hole in his chest.

She came back up to her sitting position that had her eye level with him. She leaned forward and whispered. "Can I kiss you?"

He leaned in and let her take his lips. His mouth was soft as she teased and tasted him. He close his eyes on a groan and she matched with her own. Their tongues tangled again. Her core clinched in anticipation. She had been without him too long and her body was demanding more than just his mouth and fingers. She wanted all of him.

"I need you inside me."

He stepped back, his eyes never leaving her as he unzipped his pants, took himself out and sheathed his straining dick. Her mouth watered and she saw his eyes narrow when he heard her moan.

"Come get it," he said as he stood right beneath her and eased her down on his dick supporting her thighs on his forearms. As he wedged in the tip, he looked down at them and her eyes followed. "You see how I'm stretching you out?" She whimpered and nodded, seeing how she could barely take him. "This pussy is mine." He thrusted deep, making her call out as he filled her.

He stroked so slowly, as if he wanted to savor every minute of time they had together. Their eyes were locked together. She wrapped her legs around him when he moved his arms to support her ass as he brought her down with each upward thrust.

"You're so fucking tight. You were keeping this pussy for me?" He almost snarled as he fucked her.

"Y-yes," she cried as he bounced her up and down. He bent his head, sucking the flesh of her neck into his mouth like some primal predator marking his prey. She felt like he wanted to devour her. She wanted him to. She would welcome him to feast on her. He was her soul.

He thrust up hard into her, pistonning into her pliant

flesh. She felt her nose sting as she saw the look of surrender on his face. He looked as if he found paradise. Her body clenched so tightly as she felt herself spiraling as he pounded her already sensitive tissues over and over again. Her head fell back as she broke apart.

He pulled out and turned her to the counter and thrust deep again, fucking her relentlessly. She belatedly realized he hadn't come and was desperate now for his own release. She held on to the slippery surface as he gripped her hips, pushing her into another spiral of want. He plunged deep, one hand holding her steady and the other cupping her throat.

"That's it, take this dick like you were born to do." He nipped her earlobe, his hips smacking into her. There was no retreat, only submission as he took and took what was his. Her breath caught, and he squeezed. Everything else fell away and there was nothing but the sensation left. "There you go. That's my girl," he whispered, his dick punishing, pleasuring, sending her farther than ever before. Then light taps on her clit, steady, building until waves and a crescendo of pleasure coupled with him releasing her breath erupted through her. He captured her scream, devouring her mouth as he erupted with stream after stream of his release.

He caught her in his arms sweeping her up like a bride as he strode the bedroom calling out "lights" as he went blanking the living room in darkness.

* * *

FADE WATCHED HER SLEEP. He'd not had insomnia since Delightful had come back into his life. He wondered now that she was finally in his bed for good why he couldn't sleep. They'd showered together. He put her exhausted to bed and curled his body around hers.

Thoughts of what his family would say nagged him. They were very close knit. His dad let him make his own decisions and had never interfered other than give advice based on his life experience. If he disapproved of Delightful, he would never say, but he let him find his own way. His mom was team Delightful because she knew his heart and had from the start. She'd admonished him she thought he asked something untenable of Delightful and did not think he should have held her to that promise in the first place let alone ask it of her.

Ghadi had made himself more than clear. He wanted Delightful out of his life, period. Gone was the kid who was the peacemaker. Justice's death had not only marked him and Delightful but had a dark impact on his younger brother. Ghadi was not the one to let anything slide. He only showed softness to the family. He saw FADE's willingness to forgive Didi was a weakness. He was surprised that he didn't try to oust him as CEO. Well, that would remain to be seen. He was sure to know that FADE had not come to the premier party and whom he'd left with.

His sisters loved him and wanted him happy, Flower was fierce but she was fair. Willow was Fort Knox about her own love life and extended that same grace to others. Stay out of her business and she would stay out of yours. He couldn't make that promise to her though because she was his baby sister, and he was responsible for her.

He loved them and hoped that they would be supportive, but there was no way he was willing to go the rest of his life without Delightful in his arms.

He smiled as a little snore erupted. He should tape it because she'd probably deny it.

His phone chimed. He frowned as he reached for it.

.   .   .

UNKNOWN CALLER: You saved my life once. Now I've saved yours. Stop looking into the Savelle death. He was a rabid dog, and you were his favorite bone to gnaw on. Let that sleeping dog lie.

WOW, he thought, he'd known the moment he heard that the bastard had not killed himself. Someone else had rid the world of him. Someone with enough clout to get to Savalle and to get his number.

UNKNOWN CALLER: Are we cool?

WHAT ELSE COULD he say at this point? The person had him at a disadvantage. They knew his number, and they probably knew how to get to him and his family was well. He was caught flat-footed.

FADE: Cool

ONE DAY he would know who it was but in the meantime he had to keep his family safe.

CHAPTER 21

Just Peace

Delightful walked into the sun-dappled living room. "The light is blazing against all this white." She said snuggling up beside him on the massive sofa. White and light gray on top, a deeper palette of varying purple ran the color scheme.

"You can change what you like," he murmured, head down and intently typing on the computer.

"What are you doing?"

"Recounting everything that surrounded my shooting and the areas we can build upon for CC in the future. It's for Mc2 the company shepherding us in the IPO. They want no detail left unanswered." He consulted his watch and then went back to typing.

"I'm sorry for all of this. You wouldn't need to do all of this were it not for me." The words felt so inadequate.

He turned swiftly, cupping her nape and captured her lips. They lingered for a moment. He pulled back and gave her a small somber smile. "That's the end of that. We can't move forward if you stay stuck in the past."

She knew he was right, but it smarted. There were parts of the past she was still finding it hard to shake and would take more therapy for her to come to terms with. Then his other words penetrated.

"What do you mean I can change that I like?" she laughed a little, to cover her confusion.

"What did you think I meant when I said I was done waiting?" His amber eyes were arresting in this light. They glowed like the gem and were almost luminous. He swept his hand through his curls, never breaking eye contact. She watched the locks ruffle then settle back, though looser this time. So beautiful.

"You meant we are together now." She realized immediately what that meant. "Y-You expect me to move in with you?"

"There is no expectation. It is what it is," his words were final.

She should have known he would do this. Done waiting was just that.

"You expect me to leave Lovie-Bell and Miracle?" He couldn't possibly, but he obviously did. No, this was not a test. He was calling in his marker.

"Last I checked they were grown. Miracle left y'all already and is living her best life without your constant hovering. Her words, not mine. I might add. And Lovie-Belle says there is a thing called teleconferencing when y'all collaborate. She says if she needs you on a set she's sure I will make that happen since I have a corporate jet."

"Wait a sec, you talked to my sisters? When?" She moved to stand, but he pulled her back down.

"I talked to them the night after we made love the first time." He smoothed her curls over her shoulders.

They never said anything. Probably because of what

happened right after that. Her heart plummeted. He'd been making plans for them.

"We broke up. You said I ruined everything." She felt panic seize her. She created words and worlds but found none would come when faced with what he wanted from her.

"What did I say last night?" His hand captured the side of her face. She had to face him.

"You were done waiting," she swallowed. He felt it and rubbed his thumb along the path of her neck.

"What did you say?" He whispered looking at the trail his thumb followed.

"I was done running," her words fell away as his hand dipped down over the T-shirt she borrowed.

"I like seeing you in my things, I like having you in my home. Our home. I'm going to like it when you wear this t-shirt because it's the only thing you'll be able to fit because you're full with my child," he murmured as his hand trailed further down to her belly.

"We can have that. We can build a legacy. We can do this shit right, but you have to stop fucking running every time you get scared about the future or what happened in the past. I can't fight ghosts. I've learned that. Nothing we do will bring Justice back. Ghadi is my brother, but Justice spoke to my soul. I get that. I've been hollowed out so long that I only thought you could fill me up. I was wrong about that. It wasn't until I thought you were out of my life for good that I realized that even being with you never filled me up. I had to do that shit for myself if I was ever going to be happy with you or anyone else."

She caught his hand to her heart. "I dont know what to say everything I say or do is wrong."

"You're not there yet. I've been seeing someone for years

but wasn't ready to accept it until the person I thought was going to fix me didn't."

"I'm sorry."

"Don't be I shouldn't have put that on you anyway whether or not you knew of it. That burden is too big to carry and anyone who took it on would have had a Sisyphean Task. Doom to fail."

"Why are you willing to deal with all my mess?" She threw up her hands, exasperated with herself.

"Because my family did that for me. On my darkest days, they were there. That is what family does, Didi. And you're my family now too. Miracle and Lovie-Belle said they both went to therapy, but you wouldn't after the initial grief counseling."

"I thought I should just get on with life. Live. That was what Justice is all about — moving forward. I just pushed it down and kept moving."

"Justice was a kid. He was a seventeen-year-old thinking about his dreams." He moved his hand to her shoulder sweeping up and down her arm comforting her as his gentle admonishment landed.

"You can't ascribe any wisdom to that when trying to cope with his death. He was your brother. Allowing yourself to fully grieve now is what he would want."

"I know," she acknowledged, nodding and dropping her head to kiss his knuckles on their clasped hands.

"All this time I thought I was being brave, but I was the biggest coward." Her eyes darted up to his.

"No, babe. Living at all when you wanted to curl up and die is brave. That takes more courage than anything. We made it through now, we can make it through together." She saw his eyes beseeching her. She wanted to give him the words she really did. She couldn't form the words to make him her everything. Justice had been her everything. Justice died.

"I not running…" she began.

His phone chimed. He typed something and got up. She noticed the clenching muscle in his jaw before he went to the door. He waited by the elevator and retrieved the package from the attendant, handing the young man a wad of cash.

"Big tipper. Why not use the app?" She pulled her legs under her watching as he strolled back to the sofa. He had on some low slung gray sweatpants, leaving abso-fucking-lutely nothing to her imagination.

"You are a menace." She bit her lip, looking at him.

"What? You want some?" he grinned, bringing the packages over to her.

"How could I not? I'm not a statue and if I was I'd come to life just to get some of what's swinging." She pulled him to her gripping the elastic waistband. "I owe you from last night."

"No," he said, looking down at her. Heat scorched her when his amber gaze captured hers. "Your pleasure is my pleasure. You only do what you want when you want."

"I want to," she promised, taking him out and covering him with her mouth. She looked at him through her lashes. She slowly edged him deeper. Her eyes stayed locked on his until he hit the back of her throat. He closed his eyes on a groan. His hand reached for her curls. Ever so slowly she eased him out and back again, relaxing her tongue. All the way back. Then giving a little shake of her head. She cracked her lids and saw the straining of his thighs. His sweatpants had fallen below his hips. She pulled all the way out at took his sac in her mouth and rolled him around her tongue.

"Fuck…" he groaned, holding her there to lick him. She was happy to oblige. She swirled her tongue all around before capturing him in her admittedly greedy mouth.

"Mm," she moaned, feeling her own wetness.

He pushed her back. She moved further back, taking in the view before her. His phallus jutted out hard and strong from his ebony nest of curls. The tip was broad and glistening. The sight he presented was glorious and wicked. She wanted him more than anything at the moment.

He stepped out of the pants then ripped his t-shirt over his head. "Damn." He looked even better in the broad light of day. He'd gained all his weight back and more. The leanness was still there, but it was punctuated in all the right places. Training with a professional athlete had its benefits. She had to send Marchellis a gift basket.

"Thank you kindly, ma'am." She could tell he liked the way she admired him. He reached down and pulled up the white t-shirt she borrowed and tossed it aside.

"Damn." He meant it. She saw the way his dick jumped. She lay back on his sofa. As he leaned down, pressing her body back into the cushions.

"We are going to mess up this sofa." She moaned, thinking of the white being stained. "I'll have it cleaned. Should I put plastic over it?" He smirked.

"Oh, you got jokes now?" she chuckled remembering how they used to laugh about the plastic her mom kept on her furniture.

"Yeah, but you'll be crying out for me in a second." He reached between them, touching her wetness and rubbing it over the tender flesh she'd opened so prettily for him.

"Ah," she panted, feeling his long fingers take her. He pushed deep, touching her, curving the tips just so to apply enough pressure on the nerves of the G-spot. She spread her legs wide and arched into his finger fucking crying out his name as he made her drench him and his sofa.

"You are so beautiful." He came to his knees and brought

one leg over his shoulder and eased his dick in with one slick glide.

"FADE," she cried. She could feel him so deep and in the right spot again. He kept her angled, as he took her. She arched into each thrust, grinding her pussy onto him when their bodies touched.

"So good." Her emotions were all over the place.

"Hell yes," he gritted driving home again and again. "Come for me, baby," he urged, fucking her. He stroked hard as he pressed down on her mons. She cried out her release, her back arching, her body showing him what she had been unable to say. He pulled out his dick still hard and glistening. She sat up and took him in mouth. He fucked her mouth, pushing deep again and again until he came down her throat.

"Don't you want to see what's in the bags?" he asked later once they caught their breaths. He'd pulled one of the cashmere throws over them as he held her to his chest. He kissed her forehead. He was so tender. He'd not made any recriminations about her not keeping her promise. He didn't bring up the previous conversation. She knew it bothered him, but he didn't push. That made her throat tighten. His patience was a conviction. She didn't feel worthy of the grace he was giving her. He was just loving her. No words had been spoken but who needed them when his actions said it all? She couldn't expect for him to put it out there when she'd flaked so many times. Casting pearls and all that, as her mom would say.

"Yes, I do. I guess you bought me something?" She sat up careful the thick cashmere was beneath her. They'd done enough damage to the man's, or was it theirs now?, sofa.

She opened one of the two bags. "Who told you I love Azede Jean Pierre?" She looked over to him.

"No one. I noticed you stay in her clothes. I'm a renaissance man. I know a hot look when I see it."

"Yes, but you always wear white," she mused. "Is that your brand — being pure?"

"Exactly. People equate it with purity, that's for them. For me, though, I find the absence of color calming. Muted tones and white calms my brain. I will do anything to keep my insomnia at bay. It's been better lately. Because of you. I can sleep with you."

He pulled her in his arms and into a drugging kiss.

"You barely slept last night. I'd know if you slept and your eyes have hallows." She shook her head, denying his claim.

"First night in a long time. That's about to be taken care of though." He nodded to bags.

"What do outfits from my favorite designer have to do with anything?" She crinkled her forehead curious at the guarded look that came over his face.

"Tomorrow my mom is cooking for the entire team who worked on the film." He reached out capturing one of her curly locks and swirled around his finger.

"So you are not giving them any time to adjust to the situation of us being together? They are just going to have to deal, huh?"

"Them or you?" He scoffed, and he looked away for a moment. His jaw was clinched like he was grinding glass in his molars. "I believe in starting how I plan on going forward."

She heard the cool ruthlessness in his voice. This was the guy who'd brought about a reckoning for the person responsible for Justice's death.

"At what point did I refuse to go? Can I have a chance to process?" She nudged his chest.

"Hell, no. You overthink too much." He shook his head in

a big nope way. "The next thing I know you'd be moving to Scandinavia or Australia, something like that to run away."

He laughed when she started tickling him. "Stop, Didi…" he said over peels of laughter.

"Not until you take it back." She sat back and pouted.

"Do you know how amazingly hot you look sitting there covered in cashmere, with nothing else on." He sounded as if he were in awe of her. He made her feel beautiful and wanted. *Then why won't you just be with the man?* The other her mentally yelled at her in frustration.

She leaned back into him. "Take it back." Her demand was lost on the kiss and the lovemaking that followed.

CHAPTER 22

Just Loyalty

"Are you cool?" he asked as he pulled up his car to his parents' estate in Murray Hill, a suburb in Scarsdale, New York. They'd all lived there when he first came to the city. It afforded the girls the best education money could buy once he'd hit. He'd done everything in his power to give Delightful's family the same advantage.

He knew he'd succeeded the other night when both young women were at the premier. Lovie-Belle was a stunner no matter what room she entered. She had the charisma and character that would make her a power to be reckoned with in the movie industry. Like recognized like and everything he saw, he admired — her gift and her ambition.

Miracle was a beautiful little minx, and he was proud of her. The part he played was minuscule. She'd taken the opportunity she'd been given and soared. She had created a splendid life for herself where she could use her strengths and not be penalized for her challenges.

"I'm great." She put on a good front, he thought. He'd made no moves to reassure her because to be honest he didn't know what they were walking in to. Ghadi was a wild card and Flower could still possibly go off the rails. He'd seen her talking to Delightful last night, but that was just Flower, she loved people and loved to talk. Seeing someone she knew being sat apart would never sit well with her no matter how angry she was at them.

"Good." He parked, got out then came around to open the door of the Maybach for her. She was stunning the royal blue, sleeveless Grecian sundress, that had eyelet lace running down the side.

He was in his signature white jeans and shirt, but he'd laced his Chucks to match her dress. Anyone looking at them together would know they were a couple. That small deviation spoke volumes to anyone who knew him. Never did he wear anything in public but white. This would be family, but they were posting to the Gram and Twitter accounts. This was homegrown PR made to look authentic, but there was nothing Flower did not carefully curate that made it to the public.

He stepped back, holding her arm up, their hands clasped high. Her smile was radiant as she made a slow circle for him.

"Amazing," he smiled down at her. The dress accentuated every curve underneath a diaphanous sheath.

"You don't look half bad either," she chuckled at his expression.

"I'll have you know I'm a trendsetter, woman. C'mon." He tucked her hand in the crook of his arm as they made their way up the stairs to the main entrance of his parents' home.

"Are we late?" She asked when they entered. She turned to him. There was no one to greet them.

"The guests of honor are never late." He tugged her along with him, walking through the large expanse of the living area where staff were buzzing like bees in a very active hive. They headed through the primary living area that opened onto a wide wraparound veranda. Tables were set up buffet style, but no one availed themselves of the food. The wait staff did that, taking plates laden with southern haute cuisine to waiting guests who lounged and milled around his parents' vast back lawn.

"This is beautiful." Delightful's eyes shined with pride. He wanted to take that look and hide it deep within his heart. The fact that he pleased her made his soul sing.

He drew her to him, taking her lips. She opened for him so softly, yielding her heart to him it seemed.

"Well, look who's arrived." His brother's voice called out to them. He pulled back to receive the cheers and calls from the assemble guests.

His body tensed as he watched as Ghadi strolled over to him. He knew his brother loved him and would do anything in his power to ensure his happiness. However, he would in no way allow him to denigrate Delightful.

He eased in front of her as Ghadi drew closer and saw the glint of recognition in his brother's eyes at the move. It didn't take a rocket scientist to know what that move meant, and Ghadi was a genius in his own right. He knew. So what he did next was on him.

"FADE, that's not even necessary, man." His brother shook his head as he softly chided him. "Especially after last night. May I speak to your lady?" He tilted his head to the side, trying to get a glimpse at Delightful.

He heard her gasp, then moved aside as he felt her hand press against his back. He looked down and his heart stuttered seeing the hope gleaming in her eyes.

"You see, last night I got it. I got so much of the 'Why'

between you guys. Seeing FADE through your eyes was the truest testament of love I have ever seen aside from my mom and dad and your parents. I know what you did telling your parents you felt you had to do, and that was hard. It still is, it's not for me to forgive that's up to FADE. I'm cool. FADE, bro, you know my love for you is fierce and fearless. We go hard." He stopped, his throat was working. FADE stepped to him, grabbed him hard and pulled him into his arms. "I love you, man," he whispered and pushed him back only to grab him again into a harder, tighter hug. "I love you."

"I love you too, big bro." FADE closed his eyes against the emotion cascading within him like a whirlwind.

They stepped away from each other and Ghadi turned to Delightful and held out his hand. She accepted it. The gesture was more than she could have hope for. She knew that the purity of her intention when she wrote the movie arrived with the knowledge of FADE's innocence. She wanted the world to know the man she loved. Yes, she could admit that now. Ghadi had declared it so openly, thinking she had already had the courage to say out loud what had been so clear in the movie. Pity she hadn't found the courage yet. She feared FADE's response despite his insistence that she remain by his side. She knew why he hadn't spoken those words. It has her turn. His actions had said it all.

They walked out to the guests who were congratulating them all around. She saw her sisters mingling together, Lovie-Belle supporting Miracle by holding her hand or giving her a shoulder squeeze here and there when she sensed she needed it. They both had smile infused faces. Lovie-Belle was working the crowd in the effortless, effervescent way of hers. She was in her element.

As for her she had not left FADE's side. Their interlinked hands brought smiles from his mom and dad. "You two look good together," Grace said as she bent down to kiss her on the cheek. She raised her head to see Fernando Sr. smiling in acknowledgment. "One hundred."

"Dad, don't try to get hip now, you've managed to maintain your cool by being ol'school," Willow chimed in as she squeezed herself in with the group, dragging Flower along with her. Willow gave her a hug and Flower did as well though more subdued. She didn't think it was because she was against them but missing something of her own.

The dance floor was set up with lights strung around. People were dancing to old school hip hop, shouting the lyrics to "Rapper's Delight" and pop-locking like it was yesteryear. She knew soon the cha-cha slide would break out because what gathering worth its salt did not have a cha-cha slide? major eye-roll. "FADE," she giggled as he drug her forward to dance. "Come on Didi, you know this." He grinned and her heart unfurled in an explosion love. She pulled herself together in time to perform the moves and not embarrass her very smooth partner. She couldn't have it said that FADE's girl couldn't dance. Nope. Plus, she could dance. Had even won some little group dances at the local talent show back in middle school.

Eventually the tune changed to get everyone to catch their breaths after a three track back-to-back slide remix. She knew her back was wet from the exertion. She moved but stopped when she heard the first strands of "This is Why I Love You" by Major. It felt like a reckoning. It felt like an indictment. Everything seemed to freeze in that moment. Her heart was reverberating. She could see the rise and fall of her own chest as she struggled to control herself. Then the firm hand gripping hers registered. Her gaze trailed down to the tendons of brown flesh encasing her — holding her. He'd always held her hadn't he? Lifted her. Steadied her. Loved her.

She turned into him, wrapping her free arm around him. She pulled him down so she could bury her head into his neck. She kissed him. Inhaled the powerful masculine scent of him, the clean, crisp only him scent. She wanted to bring him into her. "I found love in you too, FADE." She blinked as the tears came unchecked. "I found love with you twelve years ago. Then I hated myself so much for living when he died. He was so good. And next to him, you were what I loved most. I was scared I'd loose you too. But you never let go. You never gave up on me — on us." She pulled back to look into his eyes and what she saw there gave her hope like never before to go on. "I may never be worthy—"

"No, don't say that. You're more than worthy. Love is not about being worthy, baby. Love is about existing. I love you because you are you. You are here. I loved Justice because he was here and I will love him forever. You and me are forever too." He cupped her face and smoothed away the river of tears streaming down her face.

"We are forever," she whispered into his kiss.

*J*ust *Always*

"The wedding of the century?" Delightful turned to her sister with a look of complete shock. "Why would you say that? People are going to be comparing us to Harry and Meghan. This ain't no royal wedding!"

"Ohmygosh you know she's upset if she's slipped into AAVE," Flower peeled with laughter falling over herself on the overstuffed chaise.

Lyric shushed her, "Behave."

"Shut it," Lovie-Belle warned. "You're not our sister yet."

"Not true, technically she became our sister when they signed the marriage license," Miracle chimed in looking at her reflection. Delightful cut her eyes at her youngest sibling, knowing who she was trying to make sure she looked good for.

"She's been our sister since we were little." Delightful winked at Flower, handing her the phone to put away. She knew she could rely on her not to get it lost. Lovie-Belle would be networking as she did at all social events. The others would be having too much fun at the reception. Flower would be reliable.

"Y'all are the worst bridesmaids, by the way. You're supposed to keep me calm before I walk down the aisle, but now I'm going to be concerned with being the self proclaimed, 'Wedding of the Century'". She air quoted for emphasis dead-eyeing her all of her sisters both related by blood and not because every woman there held a significant place in her heart.

"It is the wedding of the century for the culture." Willow came to sit on the edge of the sofa. "FADE is the king of hip hop. Back on top, with his beautiful powerhouse in her own right queen." She nodded for emphasis.

"I don't like queen, too cliche," Delightful grumbled though she was wearing a tiara.

"Empress then," Lyric soothed. "Now come and put on these magnetic lashes."

Letting that thought settle in, Delightful finished her trousseau with her all sisters at her side.

"YOU SEE THAT RAINBOW?" Her dad whispered as they stood at the back of the church. There indeed was a rainbow shining over the arch where FADE stood by his father who was officiating, Ghadi, Sadiq, Marchellis, Hasan and Kris at his side.

"Yeah," her throat was already clogged with tears.

"That's J, baby. He's so happy right now, he asked the Lord to do something special for y'all." He took her hand and kissed it. "There was nothing he'd have wanted more than you and FADE to find each other again."

She took the handkerchief he offered and quickly wiped her tears as the wedding march began.

Slow, steady steps and her father holding her arm for support were the only things that kept her from running headlong into his arms. Again he was looking like a god or fallen angel come down to earth in a white tux, opened collar and the top three buttons loose with his thin platinum chains nestled within. The one that had been absent an engraving now had a D and F intertwined. He's told her when he presented her with the matching pair that he'd kept them safe for her until she was ready to receive them. Twelve years he'd held them in safe keeping for her. They lay now against her heart. He had his hands clasped in front and she had an inkling why because the dress Lovie-Belle and Flower helped her pick was gorgeous hand sewn lace and it curved to her figure like a glove. Like literally because the designer was there to make sure her couture masterpiece fit as designed. Yeah, she saw him bite his lip.

When she got to the altar one look was all it took. One look was all she needed to know that it was forever. He looked down at her with love shining in his eyes she knew he could see reflected in hers. A love that was the epitome of patience and kindness. He had not only lifted her but her family, he'd never dishonored her even when he had every right to, he'd protected her, trusted her, and in the end believed in her, his love never failed.

Finally, they would be one.

"No more running." He dipped down and pressed his head to hers.

"I'm here." She looked into his amber eyes, seeing triumph flicker.

"Just forever," he murmured.
"Just always," she promised.

"DEARLY BELOVED…"

ACKNOWLEDGMENTS

First to my husband, Christopher aka #HimDownStairs, thank you for creating the life and space that allows me to reach for my dreams. My kids aka #The3 keep being who you are. My siblings for being the first to listen to ideas and believe in me, I love you all.

Naima Simone, who told me that I have the perfect voice for Contemporary Romance, thank you for encouraging me and always being there lifting me up.

Cheryl Morgan Kennedy, who is always there sharing your incredible knowledge and critical thinking with me, I appreciate you!

La Quette, who is always there with words of wisdom, encouragement and TRUTH, you are wonderful!

Holley Trent, Adriana Herrera who read the first few pages and gave me excellent direction, y'all are the best!

The members of TheKGB thank you for giving me a place to share my love for books.

Every author, blogger and friend who has shared and supported this book, you are amazing!

Black Girl Joy Forever

THANK YOU!!!

Kenya Goree-Bell lives in Madison, Alabama with her former warrior husband and three kids. Writing as Karis Bell, she is the also the author of The Harem Diaries Series. She is a life long bibliophile and loves to talk about books. Her purpose in writing is show women as adventurous, smart and passionate. Kenya believes that Happy Ever After belongs to everyone and writes about worlds where everyone has a chance at love. She is always excited to hear from her readers!

xoxo

Kenya

https://linktr.ee/kenyagoreebell

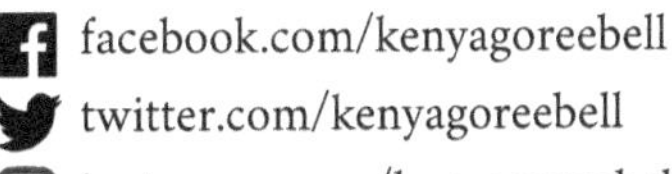

facebook.com/kenyagoreebell

twitter.com/kenyagoreebell

instagram.com/kenyagoreebell

www.ingramcontent.com/pod-product-compliance
Lightning Source LLC
Chambersburg PA
CBHW020331160726
47992CB00004B/1798